# THE LITTLE CHILDREN OF ANJENGO

# THE LITTLE CHILDREN OF ANJENGO

R. SHAMLA

PARTRIDGE
A Penguin Random House Company

**To order additional copies of this book, contact**
Partridge India
000 800 10062 62
orders.india@partridgepublishing.com

www.partridgepublishing.com/india

# CONTENTS

I dedicate my first novel to my late
beloved mother-in-law,
Mrs. Khadeeja Kunji Mohamed Kattakath

# FOREWORD

The Novel, 'The Little Children of Anjengo' by Smt. R. Shamla depicts the story of three adolescent girls, who formed an inseparable trio and were natives of Anjengo, currently known as 'Anchuthengu,' a hamlet of north-west coast of Thiruvananthapuram District. The story line is based on the life situations during the period just prior to the Indian independence. At that time this area was a British colony, not alike its neighboring villages which were parts of the Princely state of Travancore. The three girls who were pupils of Sacred Heart Middle School, run by Anglican Nuns, had vivid family backgrounds; Shama was the progeny of a feudal Brahmin family, Miley represented Latin Christian Merchants. But Cornelia, though belonged to the same community of Miley, was the daughter of a fisherman, who in essence was a member of the ordinary folk, from whom Christ chosen to become His disciples, destined to struggle in the seas to earn the daily bread with the sweat of his forehead. Cornelia was exemplarily good at studies; but was finding it tough to fully concentrate on it owing to her preoccupation with looking after the four younger ones to her and nursing her bed-ridden mother. The generosity of her soul mate shower on

9

her particularly of Shama, who in addition to her timely helps to Cornelia, persuaded her grandpa, a progressive social being to set means for the livelihood of Cornelia's family. This enables Cornelia to score a safe wicket. Towards the end, Cornelia is seen as sent for higher education in Thiruvananthpuram by Shama's grandpa. This is the crux of the somewhat elaborate narration, to put in a nut shell. The Author rightly deserves our Kudos for resurrecting a life of the bygones. We shall not miss to count the research she underwent. She succeeds in the Her clean task of translating her idea into black and white. The style is simple and transparent. The characterisation is quite impressive. I deeply appreciate the humanism expressed in the mate content of the novel. There are a lot of dramatic moments in the development of the story. Let me also point out certain points which can be useful for further improvement. There are some prosaic statements like 'Cornelia was a poor girl.' Instead of this kind of picturisation, her state of life could have been expressed comparing herself with her friends. More care should have been shown in creative situations than simply narrating facts. I think, this is the first novel written by R. Shamla. As such a lot of positive signals can be noted. She shows the energy to move ahead. I wish the writer all the best in her future endeavors.

Dr. George Onakkoor
'Sudarsana'
Nalanchira
Thiruvananthpuram 695 015
March 22, 2013

# Chapter 1

# The Little Rationalist

Shama had been waiting for her friend, Miley for the last fifteen minutes in front of the toll-booth.

The sky suddenly went dark and it started to rain cats and dogs.

The impatient Shama saw Miley running towards the ferry, covering her head with her steel school box.

It was not a cloudy day when they left home for school. So they did not take their umbrellas.

Miley got wet while Shama had taken shelter in the toll booth.

The ferry service was a boon to the Anjengo people to carry their fish products to the Travancore markets for sale.

The Anjengo backwater divided the place into two different states ruled over by two different governments.

The eastern Travancore was ruled by the Maharaja of Travancore.

The western Anjengo was under the British rule.

The people of Anjengo had to pay toll in the booth on the quay before getting on the punt to cross the backwater to their native place.

The only English middle school for girls on either side of the backwater was the Sacred Heart English Middle School in Anjengo.

The School was run by the British nuns who stayed in their convent situated near the school on the coast of the Arabian Sea.

The Sacred Heart's little children could enjoy the lullaby of both the Anjengo backwater and the Arabian Sea.

The girls from the Travancore side had to be ferried to and from school.

The School children in Malayalam schools had to begin their school work with a song praising the Maharaja of Travancore "Vanchi Bhoomi Pathe Chiram...." while the English school children in the Sacred Heart used to sing a prayer song praising the Queen of England.

"God, Save our gracious queen,

Long live our noble queen............"

Shama and Miley got impatient and waited restlessly for the ferry man to start his punt.

But he delayed in taking his pole as the downpour became heavier and the wind was getting up.

"Look at the waves in the backwater, children. It would be fool hardy to sail in a weather like this. A mistake could make the punt sink. You don't want to be drowned, eh, I wish."

The punt man's words were slurred and his yellow teeth and unpleasant smirk filled the children's hearts with hatred. But they had to take their lumps.

They gave him an icy glare.

Shama and Miley grew increasingly desperate.

They had to reach school by 9-45. The time in their wrist watches showed 9-20. Only twenty five minutes for the first bell!.

The toll collector understood the children's dilemma and felt pity for them.

He tried his best to alleviate their distress.

"Don't worry, my little ones. Your late arrival may be forgiven by the school authorities on considering the bad weather conditions. They won't punish you for your delay."

The children gave him a bleak smile. They thought:

"What does this poor fellow know about our school laws and discipline. He doesn't know that we are going to be called on the carpet for being late."

The booth man changed his conversation to encourage the spirit of the girls.

"Have you ever visited the fort of Anjengo?" He asked.

"Yes, Everyday. Our School is near the Fort. They replied with a mocking smile."

"People say that the fort helped put the place on the map. But there is a dark tunnel in the fort to go to the mid-sea where submarines arrive. The British transport India's treasures through this tunnel. You know, I'm an ardent supporter of the freedom fight going on now. I am a patriot and I want to have our freedom from the British rulers who have been draining our national wealth for many years. Indian exchequer will be depleted when we get our freedom." He said with sadness.

The girls told him that they knew nothing about the draining affairs.

Shama said, "We're deeply worried about our delay only. How can we cross the backwater and reach our school in time. That's our main concern."

The wind became calm and the rain subsided.

The ferryman called the children to come soon and get on the punt before the wind turned into another storm.

The children ran towards the punt. The wind snatched at their clothes. They held their clothes tightly and got on the punt hurriedly thanking the man.

The ferryman did not wait for other passengers. But he did not forget to give them his usual warning.

"Girls, don't dip your hands or legs in the irate water. Sharks are there to tear them off."

Miley got angry at his warning that time. She said to him in an angry mood. "This's not the time to enjoy your nasty wits. Don't try to teach your grandmother to suck eggs."

The ferryman turned his face away to hide his blushes.

He ferried them in earnest.

Their friend, Cornelia had been waiting for them since half past nine in front of the gate of the St. Peter's Church.

She had been pacing up and down desperately thinking about the severe punishment they were going to receive for their late coming.

Cornelia squinted at the heavily overcast sky.

"It'll start to rain again." She murmured.

"How can I go to school without an umbrella!? I've been entreating my father to buy an umbrella. But he always turns a deaf ear to my request."

Feeling frustrated she turned to go towards her shelter when she spotted her friends, Shama and Miley came running towards her.

Cornelia sighed with relief.

"Oh, Shama, Miley, where were you all this time? I can't count the time.

There's no sun to measure my shadow to calculate the exact time. I think it's a quarter past nine. It's late-We'd better get moving."

"No, friend. It's five minutes to ten. Let's dash." Shama said by catching her breath.

The trident had to run like mad to reach their school.

Shama, Miley and Cornelia were intimate friends.

They were studying in fifth form.

During noon break they used to sit on the bank of the Anjengo backwater watching its colour change according to the seasons, and its adoption of cruel or relaxed pose, observing the high waves rushing towards the bank to lick off the living and the non-living.

The three sang when they saw the blue water gurgling as if it were goose bumped on hearing the thrilling call of the distant firth and flowing mirthfully towards it to join her bosom friend, the Arabian Sea.

The backwater as well as the Arabian Sea was their friend, colleague and Nature coach.

Cornelia's father, Lazar was a fisherman in Anjengo.

Miley was the second child of a rich businessman in Aleppey.

Shama belonged to an orthodox Brahmin family who owned many lands and buildings in Anjengo and Travancore.

Shama's big house called 'Illam' was just a furlong away from the bungalow of Miley.

The three reached their school late by ten minutes.

Sister Benedicta, the headmistress glared at them silently for a minute.

The hostile glare in her eyes sent shivers down their spines.

She caught hold of her brutish cane kept on the table and beat Cornelia black and blue.

Cornelia wailed miserably.

Shama and Miley were sent away to their class without any punishment or warning.

Cornelia was ordered to kneel down on the veranda till she came back from her usual class rounds. Her morning and afternoon rounds and her usual surprise visits helped keep the staff and students on their toes.

Cornelia was sobbing.

Her body was racked with sobs.

The watchman, the peon, and two or three nuns who were passing by took pity on her.

The headmistress came back after her rounds. But she walked past Cornelia unceremoniously.

Cornelia glanced up quickly at her to hear an order from her to get up and go to her class. But she had a face like 'thunder'.

Cornelia felt disappointed when she saw the headmistress enter her office to tie up any loose ends.

Cornelia started to sob again.

There were red bruises on her tender hands and legs.

She felt a sharp pain in her knees.

Shama and Miley felt pity for what Cornelia was enduring.

"Poor thing!" Shama thought.

"Why didn't she beat Miley and me too? She won't beat the rich. She's afraid to touch the children from highly reputed families."

Cornelia belonged to a fishing family. She's very poor. Why does she punish only the poor girls hailing from poor fishing colony.

I hate her.

Why is it so? She's a Christian. Cornelia too is a Christian.

Their God Christ is merciful and kind-hearted. His followers too must be kind and merciful. The nuns are his saintly sisters!

"Oh! It's too cruel..........." Shama was in deep thinking.

There was a far-away look in her eyes.

"Ei, Shama! Where're you now? Aren't you in the class? Why did you come late today?" The Class teacher cried in alarm,

Shama got awakened from her deep thoughts and stood up.

She answered softly. "The abrupt shower and storm, sister."

"Okay. Sit down and listen to the lesson. Don't get immersed in your wild day dreams." The teacher gave her a harsh warning.

Shama tried her best to concentrate on the lesson but she failed.

Her mind wandered around Cornelia.

"Oh, my poor Cornelia."

Her father toils day and night in the sea for a pittance with which he tries hard to keep both ends meet.

He has to feed six stomachs at home.

His wife, Cornelia's beloved mother, has been laid up in bed due to tuberculosis.

Oh, my God! My sister, Cornelia!'"

Shama started to sob.

Sister Felistus, her class teacher rushed towards her and held her chin up and looked deep into her eyes.

"What happened to you my child?" She asked Shama very lovingly_

Shama asked politely." D'you think I could go out for a minute, Sister?" Sister Felistus's soft look turned into a harsh stare and ordered Shama to behave herself.

Shama went off the deep end and her eyes glinted.

"I must go out, I say." She screamed like an insane individual.

Shama dashed off to meet Cornelia.

The unexpected approach of Shama made Cornelia shudder and she stood up with a questioning look.

Shama grabbed Cornelia's hands and ran like the clappers towards the school gate.

She unfastened the bolted gate and both made a bolt for Anjengo Fort Court to meet her uncle in his office.

The magistrate, Mr. Raghavendra was Shama's father's first cousin.

He was holding an urgent meeting of the government officials at that time.

The police officer on duty asked them to wait outside.

The officer knew Shama well and treated the girls leniently.

The meeting was over and the police officer took Shama alone into the magistrate's chamber.

"Shama! What a surprise! Why're you here at this time? Haven't you got class? Why are you gasping and whimpering?"

Mr. Raghavendra got up from his seat and gathered her to his side and patted her head consolingly.

He looked curiously deep into her eyes.

She was crying her eyes out.

"Uncle, my friend Cornelia is standing outside. Let her also be in please." She whimpered.

Cornelia was called in.

"Why are you both weeping? Oh, the bruises! What happened to you?" The magistrate enquired.

"I wish to tell you something very serious, uncle. I'd like to share you my grievances."

The magistrate felt relieved and saw the funny side of the incident.

"Don't take it less serious, uncle. Look at Cornelia's hands and legs. The headmistress beat her black and blue, We were late for the first time in Our School life by ten minutes. Poor Cornelia was waiting for us. Miley and I were delayed to be ferried to due to storm and high waves in the backwater. After that we had to wade water-logged areas near the warehouse. It was cold and raining, and, to crown it all, we had to take shelter in a shop front and thereby we lost our precious five minutes."

Shama started crying again.

The magistrate pacified them.

"That is a fair excuse, indeed. Did you give your oral explanation to your headmistress?"

He took out his hanky from his pocket and wiped off Shama's tears from her crimson face,

"Her action was abrupt without allowing us to provide a very adequate explanation for our late coming" Said Cornelia with a mournful look on her face.

Suddenly Shama exploded with rage.

"Our headmistress is a cold-blooded monster. She punished poor Cornelia only. She should have punished Miley and me too. Why does she hate the poor and needy? She's a termite in flesh and blood to eat away the little ones' inner selves. Do something, uncle, to show that you will be able to punish her. Teach her a good lesson, uncle."

She took a few deep breaths to calm herself down.

"Oh, Shama, Come on, my dear little cherub, behave yourself and be calm and think sensibly and try to regain your self control. I know you're a genial girl. For goodness' sake, just use your common sense."

You know sister Benedicta is an outstanding and talented headmistress.

She's a strict disciplinarian. Sacred Heart is not an ordinary school, It's a British Middle School opened for teaching the British children. It's run by the English nuns who must be reverently addressed.

It's because of their kindness and pity for the backwardness of this area, they thought of admitting the local children to make them literate and thereby lead an independent life.

The Sister's commitment and dedication should be praised and appreciated.

Your headmistress had punished only Cornelia, That shows that she wants her to be more punctual and studious because her parents are backward and illiterate. They won't be able to instruct her about punctuality, discipline and good manners.

Miley and you are well refined and instead of beating you, she may inform your parents to make you punctual and disciplined. That's her best tactic to make you learn a lesson.

Now you're on trial for your double mistakes - one, your late coming; two, leaving school during working hours without the permission of the school authority.

Now the headmistress and the staff would have been searching for you.

Shama, Cornelia, go back to school at once.

Sebastian, please take these children to the Sacred Heart and ask the headmistress to get an apology from them and allow them sit in the class.

Tell her, its my order to beat the other two culprits too."

The police officer took them to school. The headmistress was standing at the gate wondering where the girls had disappeared.

The whole staff were waiting on the wide veranda looking perplexed.

They saw the court officer coming towards the gate with the children whose faces burned with Shame.

They hung their heads and dared not to face the school authorities.

The officer conveyed the magistrate's order to the headmistress first.

Then he pointed out his own views.

"His honour's niece is so kind hearted that she could not bear the Punishment meted out to her friend by you. That's why she behaved like that. She's a little rationalist." The headmistress said nothing.

"Take them to their class. No more beatings or scolding."

The headmistress expressed her regret at the incident and said with respect, "would you, please, convey my regret and apprise him to forgive me for his honour being disturbed by my school children?"

"All right, Sister. Thank you." Said the officer in appreciation of her politeness.

"That's all right, Sir." She responded.

The officer left the school.

The children were driven to the assembly hall.

She demanded an immediate written explanation and asked them to kneel on a sandy surface for half an hour.

They obeyed her order.

Her jaw was set in a determined manner.

She eyed them, her eyes ablaze with anger.

She snipped at the melting children. A mood of melancholy descended on them.

"How dare you behaved like that, You uncivilized creatures chunter about something or other. The punishment I am going to give you will act as a deterrent to other students here.

Stay on kneeling till your fatuous complaint flee from your insensitive inner self.

A circular was sent to all classes informing the staff and students to assemble immediately in the main hall.

Shama was struck by the sudden thought which reminded her of her unpardonable deed.

"Oh, God! What a grievous mistake that I did a minute ago! I jumped into conclusions again.

I left school without permission from the school authority and caused trouble to the ruler of the British area !"

Shama allowed her afflicted mind to bleed through her eyes.

She often did things without any perception.

Her instant reaction generally led her to a grievous state of mind.

She often got punishment from her kind and loving father for her thoughtless behaviour.

Her mind travelled to the U.S.A. to her father's hospital to beg his pardon.

Her mother used to advise her not to react on silly matters instantaneously.

Shama recalled her mother's words. "Think twice before you start doing anything.

Oh, God! How did this creature take its origin in my womb! Such a regardless type of ass, fly by the seat of your pants."

Her grandfather's intuitive judgement came to her help and pacified her angry mother.

He was her counsellor and his words forced her to behave sensibly.

"Kamini, you know that she doesn't like injustice. That's what that makes her react recklessly. Otherwise see her nature! She's very loving, kind hearted, magnanimous and very religious and god-fearing."

Mother always kept silent whenever her father-in-law aired his opinions.

Shama began to sob and Cornelia looked desperately at the headmistress who sat firm and kept her eyes firmly fixed on the long line of pupils coming towards the hall.

The staff and students took up their positions and the head girl, Maria Francis ordered them to stand in attention.

Sister Benedicta released Shama and Cornelia.

Cornelia was ordered to join her class.

"You must apologize to the staff and students, Shama, for your misbehaviour. You shouted at your class teacher. You ran out of the class and dashed off the school by dragging the poor, innocent Cornelia during working hours. You went to the Court and disturbed the ruler of Anjengo. This is only a small punishment. I'm not going to dismiss you because I respect your uncle and also I don't want to hurt your grandfather's feelings.

Now go to the front of the assembly and apologize."

Shama came forward with her head high and a stern look in her face.

She stood upright in front of the whole school and apologized.

She also requested the staff to pardon her and advised the students not to behave like her, to be obedient, to raise the glory and reputation of their school. The children applauded and the staff joined them.

Shama was embraced warmly by the headmistress and both of them cried for a moment.

The head girl dispersed the assembly and all the children went to their classes in silence and with relieved minds.

Cornelia went home after the class with a heavy heart.

She was the eldest of the five in her rough shelter. The thatch of the shelter was badly damaged in the rain.

There awaited a lot of domestic chores including the caring of her bed - ridden mother.

She kept her books safely in a cane basket that was hung from the supporting pole of the shelter,

She took a large earthen pot and went out to fetch fresh drinking water from the only one fresh water well situated in the compound of St. Peter's Church.

All other wells in that particular area contained only salty water which the people used for washing and cleaning.

When Cornelia reached the compound, she saw a long queue of women and children patiently waiting for their chance to draw water from the well.

Each one should bring her own bucket to draw water.

Cornelia had a bucket made out of the broad stalk of the arechnut palm.

She joined the queue and she was the last one to get a chance.

When she reached home with the heavy earthen pot full of water on her head, Alex, her first brother, ran towards her to help in bringing the pot down on the kitchen floor.

Alex always helped Cornelia in cleaning the house and washing the vessels. Some times he fetched firewood and dried coconut leaves for lighting fire in the hearth.

Alex was ten years old.

Cornelia's second brother, Joseph, who was the spitting image of his father was eight years old.

Her first sister, Mary's age was four and the last one, the little Lily was only two years old.

All the five were strikingly good looking and well-mannered.

Cornelia cooked tapioca.

She made a tasty fish dish. The children had a wash and came in and sat on the floor in a line.

Cornelia dished out the items.

Lazar came home late because he had to get medicine for his wife from a village physician far away.

He brought some rice and a little oil in a small bottle.

His black and curly hair was smeared with oil and he went out to have a bath in the backwater near the ferry service.

On his way to the bathing place he began to muse about his wife's fate and to muse on the events at sea, worry about his difficulty in the upbringing of his five little ones and at last he thought about the one meal of the day.

He rushed home after the bath. His stomach was calling aloud for food.

Cornelia had already cooked the rice and waited for her father.

She dished out a plateful of rice and another earthen plateful of tapioca with fish curry.

Cornelia requested her father, "Please come in father, and sit down and take the weight off your feet for a moment."

Lazar obeyed her.

He sat down on a mat.

Cornelia placed the plates of food in front of him.

Lazar prayed. He was so hungry that he devoured the whole without taking a single moment to chew the food.

He wiped his hand across his mouth, then belched loudly.

Cornelia, Alex, Joseph, Mary and Lily dissolved into laughter when their father belched.

Cornelia then went to attend to her sick mother.

Mother was helped to sit. She sponged her mother's weak body using a soft towel and warm water.

Mother was fed and was laid down gently on the bed.

Her sick body was covered with a battered blanket.

Cornelia was only twelve years old. But she did the chores as if she were a matured woman.

Her mind and her body were strong. Her hard work was appreciated by the fishing folk of Anjengo.

She was fair, beautiful and chummy.

Her attractive appearance reminded the people of Anjengo of the holy face of Madonna in pictures which they keep in their homes for worshipping.

Her mother's illness, the caring of her siblings gave her a hard time at her joining school. She was seven when she was admitted in 1st form.

\* \* \* \* \* \* \*

# CHAPTER 2
# CORNELIA'S DREAM

The shelter was too small to accommodate all the seven members.

Cornelia slept on a mat spread on the floor under her mother's cot with her two younger sisters, Mary and Lily.

Mary and Lily went to sleep after having their supper.

Cornelia studied her lessons and finished her homework.

After her school work she went to sleep.

Cornelia was in fifth form. She had to study a lot because the Sacred Heart followed the British Curriculum.

She used to burn the midnight oil in order to complete her daily portion and her revision of earlier lessons.

The only light she had in the room was from a kerosene oil lamp which gave out both light and black smoke.

In spite of all severe disadvantages she used to have straight A's all through Primary and Middle School.

Because of the scarcity of space in the shelter Lazar used to sleep on the veranda of Prakasi Akka.

Prakasi Akka was an old woman of seventy living alone in her big house which was very near to Lazar's shelter.

She was running a coffee shop with all kinds of eatables like bread and soup; boiled tapioca with fried fish; rice and fish curry and so on and so forth.

The fishermen, fish - mongers, the women of Anjengo, poor school children hailing from the colony, and sometimes working men and women were her customers.

People used to sit on the mats spread on the wide veranda facing the Arabian sea and enjoy their food. They could see the waves breaking on the shore; the seagulls dancing on the waves and the fishermen pulling their nets. The soft sea breeze fanned them to cool.

There would be a big rush in her coffee shop when the fishermen got a good catch. The old woman was very strict in her dealings. She had never given credit and she was a loan shark too.

The veranda of Prakasi Akka at night was a haven of peace and tranquility to Lazar.

There was a sort of symbiotic relationship between Lazar and Prakasi Akka.

By sleeping there on the veranda Lazar got rest and sleep at night without anybody's interference or sleep impediment. At the same time the lonely woman felt safe and she would not be afraid of burglars or hooligans at night.

Lazar had such a strong physique of a hard working fisherman that nobody would ever be dare enough to face him.

Cornelia went to sleep at half past eleven.

In her sound sleep her mind fell into the trap of a delirious dream.

She was in the attire of the wife of the District Magistrate of Anjengo.

She wore a twinkling hip chain over her golden colour sari.

Her traditional neck chain and wedding band were glittering as they were studded with diamonds. They were shown a flashlight around the passers-by.

She had a jasmine garland coiled round her dark curly locks.

Her nose ring sent out flashes when she smiled at people who bowed their heads in respect for the ruler's wife.

Men, women and children of Anjengo liked her sapphire eyes, dimpled cheeks and her graceful walk.

People used to gaze at her in admiration while she was strolling along the beach on week-ends. At times she distributed sweets to the poor children of the fishermen of Anjengo.

Cornelia's sweet dream got broken and she began to shudder at the appearance of sister Benedicta swirling her creamcoloured brutal cane in the air and snarling abuse at her.

Cornelia screamed out in terror.

She woke up from her sleep.

Her body was damp with perspiration.

She searched her body for her dress and ornaments. But all disappeared.

The jasmine garland which was adorning her hair, her glittering hip-chain, and the diamond necklace vanished. She felt her body for her ornaments.

Her hip-chain shattered to pieces.

Her diamond necklace was hurld.

Her body was bare.

Cornelia looked around and her eyes fell on the faces of her sisters. She sounded relieved when she saw them in deep sleep.

But Cornelia's mother called her in a faint voice.

"Corne, Corne, what happened?

Did you scream in your dream, dear?

Pray to Jesus and you may get good sleep without any bad dreams."

Cornelia did not answer her mother and kept silent for her mother to fall into a sleep.

But she could not sleep after that bad dream. She had to lie sleepless until dawn by recalling her fantastic dream.

The next morning, while they were on their way to school Cornelia told Shama and Miley about her mind blowing dream.

"Yesterday's nightmare makes me feel strange even now, my friends.

I had a strange dream last night."

Cornelia started describing what she had dreamt.

Shama interrupted Cornelia.

"Don't say anything about what you had dreamt. Dreams should be kept secret."

Cornelia anxiously enquired.

"Why Shama? What's the matter?

Why should dreams be kept secret?

Why can't I share you?"

"Because letting it out may put you in troubles. It would hurt you in one way or other." Shama warned her.

"Who told you all these false beliefs?" asked Miley with scorn.

"My servant, Kalyani told me. She's an expert palmist and dreamologist." Shama said by raising her eyebrows.

"Dreamologist! Are you coining new words, Shama?" Cornelia asked mischievously.

"She's coining new words like the word 'cardboard city which means, homeless people living in cardboard boxes." Milie ridiculed Shama.

"My Kalyani is an expert dream analyser." Said Shama firmly.

"Pooh! She's indeed a deceiver. Corne, you please go on with your dream. I'm all ears." Miley encouraged Cornelia.

"I want to share all events and my experiences whatever they may be with my bosom friends. So, Shama, with your kind permission I'm going to describe my dream and my late-night shuddering." Cornelia looked at both in eagerness.

"Shuddering!" They exclaimed in unison.

"Yes, friends. "Then Cornelia described what she had dreamt.

Shama and Miley listened carefully to her description with joy and wonder.

"Take it from me, friends. Cornelia's dream says that she'll be the wife of a very rich man. Miley prophesied with her trademark smile.

Shama interfered and remarked "Oh, the other way round too. She'll be the wife of an idiot. You know Miley, dreams are nothing but a person's mind slide. It recalls what a person sees and experiences during day time. Corne is poor. She often sees my aunt in glittering attire and jewellery and her unattainable attractiveness, her stylish ways were stamped deep in Corne's inner mind.

The bitter experiences at school made her inner self hurt a lot. All these beautiful and bitter thoughts flashed back to her through her dream.

Pray well before you go to sleep. Then there'll be no dreams at all; no more nasty visions.

We are the children of the sacred Heart in Anjengo. We must work hard and we must try to attain a lot in life through our great diligence, dedication and commitment to our studies.

Cornelia, please don't believe in Cinderlla's dream and think that no one can be a princess if only one dreams.

We can be princess through our hard work. Let us try our level best to attain our goal.

Now come on friends, move fast. We don't want to repeat the traumatic experience that we underwent yesterday."

They walked fast. But Miley and Cornelia looked at each other and showed eyebrow signs in appreciation of their friend's pithy observation and philosophy of life.

Miley expressed her admiration.

"You talk like a rationalist. You seem to be a bit of a philosopher. If you don't mind, tell us, from where you got these high life ideals.

"From my grandfather, a hale and hearty person. A great man of efficiency and he is an egalitarian too." Shama responded.

"What does the word 'egalitarian' mean? Cornelia asked Shama anxiously.

"Egalitarian means a person who believes in equality. No rich, no poor. All are equal and must enjoy the same rights and opportunities". Shama explained.

"A very nice gentleman indeed. Can I have a chance to meet him? Would you please take us home to have a look at that mentor?" Cornelia requested Shama.

"That's impossible Corne. It'll be a difficult attempt to meet my grandfather. It's very difficult to get into my house.

There's a devil called untouchability guards the house. It won't allow you in. My grandpa is quite okay. He's a likable man. Miley had many chances to meet him and talk to him outside, either on his way to the temple or on the field while he was giving instructions to the workers there. But other family members won't allow you in." Shama said in a soft voice.

"But why is it so?" asked Cornelia grievously.

"It's because you are a 'Nasrani' and they are Adya Brahmins. Gandhiji tried to evict this demon from upper caste houses but some are still keeping the demon to guard the big door way of some strict Brahmins." Shama said in an angry way.

"Who are you, then? You said 'they' instead of 'I'. Miley asked with a smile. "I'm a human being. I've no caste and creed. Discrimination of any sort is abhorrent to a civilized society. To me-no big-no small, no rich-no poor.

I believe in only one God, the almighty.

That God cannot be depicted. Idols and deities cannot represent the Almighty. Yet I go to temple to worship the deities there to please my parents and relatives.

I respect your Jesus Christ because he had lived and sacrificed and got crucified for a good cause.

I have great respect for Mohamed Nabi for his endeavour in establishing a new religion and presenting the world a religious text to spread the word of God, the message of Islam.

"Have you read and got the ideas from the religious books of Bible and Quran, Shama?" asked Miley with wonder.

"No, not yet. Grandpa only told me about Christ and Mohamed while he was reciting Bhagavad Geetha and Ramayana.

"What's your own God's nature then? Whose image comes into your mind while you pray in a temple?" Miley asked.

"Sorry Miley? I can't explain. My God is something indescribable.' Very holy, indeed! That's in my heart's inner sanctum-sanctorum." Shama expressed her views very piously.

They reached school in time. The headmistress ordered them to join the prayer group.

Miley was the head singer as her voice was melodious and she led the group. She used to give practice to the group.

Shama and Cornelia were very weak in singing. They could only move their lips while others sang the prayer song louder.

Shama and Cornelia often praised Miley that she would be a great musician one day.

Their first period was their best period, Children loved that period as it was handled by sister Alfonza, a sweet angel like nun who loves all children. She took English in all fifth Form divisions. She was an expert in handling English Language and Literature.

When she taught them Shakespear's drama, the scenes from the play were enacted by her to impress the children and make them learn it in an interesting and easy way.

All were absorbed in the lesson and learnt it immediately with a great deal of admiration and palatability. So the children loved sister Alfonza's English class and they used to await for her arrival in the class eagerly.

The second period was the most horrible one. Most of the children in fifth form hated that period.

Sister Martha's Mathematics period created a kind of negativity in the minds of the backward children. So they hated the teacher and nicknamed her as Sister Masda instead of Martha - Multiplication, Addition, Subtraction, Division, Accuracy.

The severest and the hardest period is the second period.

Sister Martha's serious figure and her stern face made her children's blood freeze.

She was a virago in the school episode.

She came to her class with her brutal cane swirling and swishing in the air with a heavy face full of wrinkles around her eyes and forehead.

Her eyeglasses always rested at the tip of her aquiline nose. She gave the children her stare just over the glasses not through them.

She went round the class to pick out those who were doing the sums incorrectly or those who sat inattentive in the class and pinched them hard on their ears.

The inattentive children and the mischief makers were commanded to stand up and turn to show their back to get the cane. These children then thought of wearing thick panties made of hard denim to avoid bruising.

Cornelia was loved by sister Martha for her brilliance in Maths and she always scored hundred out of hundred.

Miley too scored high in mathematics.

Shama was only average in Maths. She often neglected the subject because she was a little lazy to go through the Mathematics lessons.

One day Sister Martha summoned Shama to appear before her.

She advised her a lot to give more attention to her subject too.

"You are demeaning me by neglecting my subject alone. Give a little more time to practise Maths at home. It's an easy and interesting subject if you go thoroughly through it and repeatedly practise it. Try your level best and see and enjoy the fruit of your hard and sincere work. I wish I could see you in the first place next time.

Shama was not like the other average students who hated Maths and the Maths teacher. She often scolded Shama and gave her nice beatings. But she loved the sister for her dedication and sincerity.

Shama's average performance in Maths was not only sister Martha's but also other teachers' despair.

So she agreed to follow sister Martha's advice and promised her that she would come first in Maths in the second term exam.

When Cornelia came to know of her promise to sister Martha she laughed at Shama and tried to challenge her.

"You can never beat me in Maths, You better take that pot of water off your hearth."

Shama retorted by ridiculing Cornelia. "Let's see Corne. Cool your heels".

There started a constructive competition between the two. She could soon get ahead of others in her class.

Shama got hundred out of hundred in Maths in the next exam while Cornelia got only ninety nine out of hundred.

That day, during lunch break Cornelia gifted Shama with a walletful of broken glass bangles of different colours which she had collected and kept in her shelter for making chains.

"What's this Corne?" asked Shama with anxiety.

"Broken glass bangles of different colours. We can make chain by heating and bending each piece.

I'll show you. Let's go and sit under the bread-fruit tree.

Cornelia took out a candle and lighted it and kept it in the sand.

Then she took out a red colour glass bangle piece and holding the two ends between her thumb and forefinger and showed the middle portion to candle to get it bend due to heat. She, then pressed the ends together to form a curved shape. Then she made a chain out of the heated links.

On seeing that long colourful glass chain Shama got very excited and pressed the chain on to her bosom with her eyes full of tears of happiness.

"It's a gift to you, Shama, as I have nothing precious to present you". Cornelia said with heart felt satisfaction.

"But why do you give me a present now?" asked Shama.

"Because you beat me in Maths. Now I know that nothing is difficult for you, my friend. You're a genius! Keep it up."

Cornelia embraced Shama. Miley was coming running towards them and without knowing the reason she too joined them in hugging.

They three stood in a trance for a minute.

Shama stretched out her right hand and showed Miley her present from Cornelia.

Miley took the glittering chain in her hand and asked Shama, "For what?"

"For beating Cornelia in Maths."

Miley made fun of Cornelia.

"If I were you I'd hate my rival."

"That's what my Corne! She's different. She's my sweet little sister. We're one. Nobody or no good cause can break our friendship. Said Shama.

They three had their lunch under the green foliage. Shama and Miley shared their food with Cornelia who had no food of her own in the afternoon.

They rested under their beloved bread fruit tree after their lunch and Miley sang melodiously to please her friends.

\* \* \* \* \* \* \*

# Chapter 3
# The Bread Fruit Tree

The broad leaves of the Breadfruit tree formed a green dome and shaded the little children of the Sacred Heart from the hot sun.

The green leaves shook with laughter while listening to the merrymaking of the little innocents playing under her.

They played various games in the bower during their recess.

In February and early March the stalks bore pot-like fruits which attracted the children and they danced in accordance with the movement of the dangling fruits from the tips in soft breeze.

They used to clean the ground under the tree by sweeping or hand picking the fallen leaves, twigs and fruits. They carried the wastes in the baskets and put them in the compost pits in order to study how organic manure was prepared.

Nature study was one of the subjects apart from Home science and public health they had to study.

The ground was always kept clean so that they could loiter under the tree in a clean and green atmosphere.

The nuns would often come out and stood watching the little butterflies at play or work and at times joined them in their games.

The Sacred Heart English Middle School in Anjengo was very particular and strict about the students' cleanliness, hygiene and discipline.

Pupils were taught about the importance of personal hygiene.

Pupils from the fishermen's colony were specially attended by the nuns to make them wash their hair full of lice and nits. Their lice-ridden hair was washed with carbolic soap and warm water.

Each one was supplied with a basin full of warm water to wash their hair and clean their mouth.

They were kept in a line facing a tripod stand on which was kept a basinful of warm water, carbolic soap and a clean dry towel.

They followed the instructions of the public health teacher sister Nancy about how to wash their hair.

This ordeal was a common sight on all Wednesdays under the bread fruit tree.

Cornelia was exempted from this washing episode as she used to come to school very neat and tidy.

Miley and Shama gave Cornelia their fresh, clean and neat hand-me-downs to wear in school. She kept apart the Sunday best for special occasions.

She used her friends' white silk frocks to wear when she goes to the church-services.

Miley's mother often gave Cornelia new sarees for her mother.

Even Lazar was presented with Miley's father's pants and coats, shirts and trousers after one or two uses.

But Lazar found them luxurious and also he was not in the habit of wearing them. So he used to present these costly items to the peons or watchmen of the court and they in return presented Lazar with new loin clothes.

Miley's mother sent milk, eggs and sometimes soup to feed her sick friend who once was her classmate and friend. They were choir-girls of St. Peter's.

Lazar showed his gratitude by presenting big and tasty fish to Miley's father free of charge from his catch.

School was closed for the summer vacation.

Shama, as usual, went to Bombay to spend her holidays with her cousins, Gaya and Gauri, her fraternal uncle and her maternal aunt.

Shama's uncle Shiv was her father Vishnu's younger brother.

Shama's aunt Visakha and her mother Kamini were twins.

Every year Shiv and family came home to spend their Onam holidays and Shama was taken there to Bombay to spend her summer vacation with them.

Miley spent her vacation in Ooty where her grandparents lived'

So Cornelia felt so lonesome during the long vacation missing her bosom friends for more than fifty days.

But she had a lot to do at home. She was fully engaged in serving her sick mother, feeding her younger ones, helping her beloved father in either repairing his net or in spreading the fish on the hot floor of the coast under the hot sun to get them dried.

The Sacred Heart was reopened after the long vacation.

The very first day gave them an extreme shock to the little children of Anjengo.

Their beloved bread fruit tree had been cut off and in its place they could see a lifeless building named 'Tailoring and Embroidery Block.'

Shama grieved the loss of the tree. It was a treasure and the children loved the tree more than anything else in Anjengo.

"Why did the nuns cut off and sold the precious living being which even gave them good yield every year? The children asked one another.

The big pot-like fruits were of high demands in the market of Travancore and the nuns used to get nice profit from their sales.

Shama looked at the stone building and shed tears over the loss of her tree friend.

The three friends sat in gloomy silence on the round rock near the bank of Anjengo backwater.

They observed the silently flowing water.

It seemed to them that the water too was grieving at the loss and flowing towards the firth to convey her friend, the Arabian Sea, about her daughters' loss of their benign tree friend.

"Look at the backwater, friends," Cried Shama, "no one can sell her. She'll be there for ever and continue flowing without anybody's interference. We can enjoy' her beauty till we breathe our last.

Miley murmured, "How could they cut the tree off so mercilessly. They could have built the block somewhere in the northern side without destroying the big tree. So cruel are those nuns, especially the mother superior. She's only after money. These Westerners don't know the value of trees. They expect a good income from the new set up. They might have understood the value of trees and plants. They are valuable as well as knowledgeable.

Cornelia exploded with rage, "If I had had a gun in my hand I would have shot the nuns on sight. I want to eat them alive."

Miley explained with a lot of emotions "The tree was like a mother to us. She was carrying hundreds of pots in her hands looking at us smiling and murmuring soft tunes in our ears to make us relax under her, patting us with the soft breeze to make us feel sleepy under her.

It was a suitable place for our silent study during exams. It was an important place for our merrymaking and enjoyment during our recess."

Other students too shared the same feeling with Shama, Miley and Corne. They too expressed their expostulation about the destroyal of the tree.

One day Shama asked the gardener by looking at him squarely.

"Why didn't the sisters build the new block somewhere else on the southern part where there are no trees?"

The man with schadenfreude answered.

"Oh, the useless tree was a nuisance to us. It was old enough to be cut down.

But the main reason was that the carpenter, when measured the area for the block, proposed that the place where the tree stood, was suitable for building in accordance with the lay-out and the nature of the earth science.

The institution is going to be beneficial not only to the Anjengo women but also to the Travancore house wives.

There's a rush to get admission here. You know, the Travancorean house wives swarm the block to seek admission.

My wife too is a candidate and she was called for an interview next Saturday." The gardener had a very high opinion of the nuns' endeavour to start a vocational training centre for the women.

Shama lost her temper with the man and shouted at him.

"But this is an English School for girls. This will become a fish market then.

The peace and serenity of this educational institution will be destroyed by the bustling and chattering of those uneducated and uncultured women."

Miley asked him whether the nuns were going to levy high fees for the course. "No, Missie; not of course. Only affordable fee. After the course the women can earn a living as seamstresses."

Shama got so angry that she stuck her tongue out at the poor fellow and scolded him a lot for being on the nuns' side.

The gardener got upset and stood silently for a minute looking at Shama, whom he considered to be high-born and a plutocrat.

"Why are you angry, Missie? You only asked me. Did I say anything wrong to hurt your feelings? The man stood toneless and he felt ashamed.

"No, no, Joseph. Don't feel like that. We are very sorry for the loss of our beloved bread fruit tree. That's why she's angry. Please pardon us." Miley intuited that they were badly wrong.

They went to their class.

Shama could not listen to the lessons.

Her mind wandered around the tree.

"Ei, Shama, Are you in a dream world'?" Sister Lucy threw a piece of chalk at her to make her alert and sit attentive in the class.

"Come on, stand up and answer my question. How do leaves make starch?"

"Oh, Mam! Leaves are no more to make starch. Everything had been cut off by you and your comrades." Shama answered sadly and she began to cry her eyes out.

The astonished Sister Lucy went to her and wiped off her tears and asked Miley what had happened to the girl.

Miley explained everything and other children too aired their objection to the cutting off of their friendly tree.

"We have a strong sentimental attachment to the bread fruit tree." The children said.

"We are all utterly bereft when the tree was cut off."

The sister laughed and told them to think sensibly.

"Don't be silly, children. There are plenty of saplings in the compound. Root out some of them and plant them in your compound. They'll grow soon. You know breadfruit trees are not so useful as Teak, Rosewood or other strong timber. You know Shama you're simply wasting my time on a good for nothing tree.

Sister Lucy looked at her watch impatiently and asked them to listen to the subject.

Shama obeyed her teacher and listened to the lesson well and answered her questions.

During noon break, the three thought of visiting Lady Mary, a white lady who lived in a big bungalow near the fort. Her compound was full of sweet-smelling plants and big fruitbearing trees. They used to visit the kind young English lady, her mother and her cousin.

"We'll meet Lady Mary in the afternoon. The trees and plants in her compound will give us some Solace and also we can share our griefs with her." Said Shama to her friends.

"Okay, Shama. We can go there after our lunch. I wish to see the Magnolia there. Miley and Cornelia agreed.

"Let's forget about our lost bread fruit tree by looking at the greenery there." Said Cornelia.

They went and sat on the veranda of the Home Science Block and had their food,

Cornelia was served with rice, curd and a banana by Shama and Miley gave her slices of bread with butter and jam.

Shama was a pure vegetarian. Miley too would bring only veg items after the first day's incident in school.

On the first day Miley brought a beef-steak and a beef burger in a bread roll.

Shama saw this and the smell which was unfamiliar to her made her vomit a lot.

The vomiting continued till she fell unconscious in the class.

She was admitted in a distant hospital and was under treatment there for a week.

The sisters then ordered the children to bring only vegetarian food to school. After their lunch the three-ran towards the fort to meet Lady Mary,

Her bungalow was always spick and span.

The English family welcomed the children very warmly.

"Hello, my little butterflies! How're you?"

"We're fine. Thank you." They responded frankly.

"Why such a visit this time? Have you had your lunch? "Lady Mary asked them.

"Yes, of course, Mam.

We came here to enjoy the scenery here. We want to smell the fragrant flowers and the eye-catching greenery to shed our grief over the loss of our dear bread-fruit tree in our school compound."

"What happened to your breadfruit tree, children?"

"The sisters cut it off to build a new block there." Shama unfolde her grievances.

Lady Mary sat in silence enjoying the ebb and flow of their conversation, At last she said smiling.

"Oh, my little children, breadfruit trees are not so valuable. Their fruits are okay. But their wood is not valuable, There's nothing to worry about its loss.

"Come on, trident, I'll show you a special plant in my garden, I brought it from Mysore two years ago."

"Madam, d'you know what's meant by the word 'Trident'? Shama asked Lady Mary with a sweet smile.

"Yes, dear. I know. The word means that a trident is a three-pointed weapon of your god, 'Shiva'. It looks like a long fork with three sharp points-Shama, Miley and Cornelia are the three sharp points in one human fork; allright?

The Children laughed.

Lady Mary took them to her back garden and showed the plant with green broad leaves and hanging blooms.

The children stood awestruck and inhaled the smell of the blooms permeated the air around them.

Lady Mary's cousin came out of her room and shook the branches to let the sweet smelling flowers fall to the ground.

The children ran towards the flowers to gather them.

While rushing towards the plant Miley fell over Lady Mary's furry cat which was lying in the garden.

Shama and Cornelia began to laugh.

Miley stood up and announced that she did it purposely to make them laugh. The cat was staring at Miley and she stuck her tongue out at the staring cat. All had a good laugh.

The three then began to collect the fallen flowers and kept them in their pockets to take them home.

Then they visited Lady Mary's bed-ridden mother and greeted her warmly, She was a lady of advanced years.

"Good afternoon, Madam. We pray for your speedy recovery. May God bless you with good health and a long life." They wished her in unison.

"Thank you girls." The old lady smiled at them.

"The little Indians are always welcome to my house. When I see you, I feel a little better. Mary, give them the biscuits which Thompson had brought from England last week," Lady Brijitha told Mary.

"Madam, we came here to get peace and relaxation to our troubled minds. Now we are quite all right. We feel enthusiastic and sturdy. Thank you all." Said Shama.

While Lady Mary was going inside to get the biscuits, they heard the gong of the Sacred Heart. They dashed out of the house like a wind without waiting for the biscuits,

The headmistress saw them running towards the school.

She doubted nothing this time as it was their usual trip at noon to the court to meet Shama's uncle.

Now they came to know of their act of sheer folly and tried their best to give their full attention to their studies.

Through their wide reading, constructive discussion and laudable seminars the three became the real gems of the Sacred Heart English Middle School, Anjengo.

\* \* \* \* \* \* \*

# Chapter 4
# Death Rattle

The Sacred Heart remained closed for a week due to torrential rain, strong wind and flood.

Almost all parts of the village remained heavily water logged.

It had been raining incessantly since the fifteenth of February.

It was unusual for the Nature to rain in February.

Strong winds accompanied by heavy rain, thunder and lightning swept through the place.

It was a terrible night. A gale started blowing fearfully. There was trouble looming on the horizons.

A loud thunder startled Lazar and he got up suddenly and ran home.

Cornelia was sitting beside her mother gathering the four towards her breast.

The five were shivering and shaking with fright. Lazar ran to them.

He took his wife with both hands and put her on his broad shoulder. He then gathered his children and dashed out of his dilapidated shelter.

He reached the veranda of Prakasi Akka.

He laid his wife slowly and tenderly on his mat.

No sooner had they reached the veranda than they heard a loud crash and saw their hut in flames due to a peal of thunder and a flash of lightning.

Prakassi Akka opened her door and looked at the fire trap and shuddered. Soon she sent out a sigh of relief when she saw Lazar and family on the veranda.

She took her hurricane lamp and showed them the way to an inner room.

The sight of the sick woman and the fright in the eyes of the five little ones made her-rush to spread a bed sheet on the divan there and asked Lazar to take his wife from the damp floor to the divan. She took out her best blanket to cover her body.

Lazar and children were given enough mats and sheets and pillows to sleep comfortably in the inner room.

Cornelia was provided with a bed pan for her mother's use. Lazar thanked her with tears in his eyes.

The vicissitudes of his family life made Lazar heavy and upset.

The poor soul now cursed God and he stretched his eyes beyond the unbridled sea with high waves breaking hard on the shore.

Cornelia saw her mother vomiting blood.

"Father, look, Muma's vomiting blood. She shouted and began to cry aloud. The children let out a scream of fear and Prakasi Akka came back running from her room.

Cornelia cleared the divan and cleaned her mother's face off blood still crying in grief. But her mother continued vomiting blood till she went into a coma.

Morning arrived with horrible news of destruction and a horrible natural calamity that played havoc throughout the area.

Wild storm, thunder and lightning took a heavy toll on the people's huts and fishing equipments.

Many became homeless and the trees and plants were burnt down by thunder bolts.

Nothing daunted the people set about rebuilding their shelters.

People were provided with temporary shelter in the Parish hall and in school buildings.

The British government extended their help to the fishermen who had lost their shelters, fishing boats and nets on a war footing.

They built rows of make shift huts for the homeless on a temporary basis.

Prakassi Akka did not allow Lazar and children to move elsewhere. She ordered the family to stay there and they were provided with enough food without showing any hesitation.

She loved Lazar as her own son.

The Earth completely regained her calmness after a sheer weather turmoil and unsteadiness by the twentieth of February. Cornelia's mother stayed in coma for a week.

The Vicar of St. Peter's church visited her and offered a special prayer as she was clearly sinking fast and was nearing death.

Lazar and children stood around her sinking body and wept uncontrollably. Nobody could console them.

The school started to work again when the flood waters gradually subsided.

Shama and Miley heard the news of their friend's pitiable condition.

They called on Cornelia in the morning on twenty first February.

The piteous sight of Cornelia's mother made their eyes filled with tears.

They saw Alex and Joseph sitting in a corner resting their heads on their knees and whimpering.

They had no words to console them.

Miley looked around. She watched the weeping willows shedding tears. Miley felt so sad that she went near the boys and patted their heads consolingly and lovingly.

They saw Cornelia's mother breathing hard and they could hear the death rattle from her throat. Shama and Miley got frightened at the sight and embraced Cornelia for a support. Cornelia was wailing with her eyes fixed on her mother's face. She clutched her mother's hands to her and called her "Mumy, Mumy, don't go mumy."

Shama and Miley took Cornelia's hands in them and tried their best to console her. But no one could bear the loss of one's mother. So they let Cornelia cry her eyes out. At last Cornelia's mother came to an untimely end. She was only twenty eight years of age when she died.

Lazar was broken hearted.

The five wept bitterly.

The fishermen, their wives and children of Anjengo came running towards the house to mourn the death.

Lazar and his wife's relatives, parents and friends arrived soon.

They were discussing the funeral function.

The body was taken to the funeral home to wash and to be prepared for being buried. Visitors were allowed to see the prepared body.

Cornelia lost her mind for a while and uttered to her friends.

"My muma died. We lost everything -our home, our things, our hopes, everything. We must end our lives in the Arabian Sea. It's she who feeds us, she who cares us; she who looks after us. She can very well take away our lives.

Cornelia leaned on Shama's shoulders and wept her heart out.

Miley put a consoling arm around her shoulders and said.

"There's nothing we can do about our fate, Corne! We'll just have to grin and bear it.

Cornelia fell into a bottomless pit of sorrow.

The sky grew dark and suddenly it began to rain heavily.

The two little sisters of Cornelia shuddered with fear.

Miley took Lily in her hand and held her tight to her chest while Shama cuddled Mary to make her calm and quiet.

The sea groaned as if the sea god had hit her on her head when she did not expect a strike at that moment.

The sky hurled sharp needles of rain upon the earth and the earth got hurt, soaked and shivered.

Miley and Shama left the house when it stopped raining.

Lazar's parents and relatives shared the funeral expenses and many extended their support to Lazar in his difficult and unhappy situation.

It was a heart breaking scene to find Lazar sitting in a corner still and stone like.

After a day's mourning the remains of his beloved wife and his five children's loving mother was buried in the cemetery of St. Peter's Church in a befitting manner.

Days passed

Little by little Lazar and children tried to recover from their grief stricken situation.

One day Lazar was called by Shama's grandfather to his barnyard and asked him about his stay in Prakassi's and about his future plans.

Lazar was granted permission to build a small stone house of his own on grandpa's property on the south coast of Anjengo just behind the fort.

Grandfather provided Lazar the necessary building materials, workers and a building contractor to build a two bedroom stone house for Lazar and children to live in. He was a good sport.

A small stone house with two bed rooms, a kitchen, a small work area, a veranda and a small store house for Lazar to keep his nets, fishing equipments and dried fish at the back of the house was built within two months and presented it to Lazar and his children.

Lazar and children moved to the new house which was purified and blessed by the vicar of St. Peter's church.

Now Lazar and his children could stretch themselves out inside their own abode without any fear of eviction.

Grandpa gave Lazar the legal documents regarding his ownership of the five cents land and the house on it.

Lazar knelt down and bent his head to touch his head on grandpa's feet and washed them with his tears in respect and gratitude "I owe you a great debt of gratitude. May God bless you and your great family with long healthy lives and prosperity.

Grandpa ordered Lazar to put his shoulder to the wheel again and bring up the five little children well.

Cornelia was asked to attend her school from the next day onwards.

Miley's father helped Lazar by giving him furniture and a small sum of money to meet his household expenses till he began to go fishing again.

Prakassi Akka presented Cornelia with the divan on which her mother breathed her last peacefully.

Cornelia kissed the divan many times as if she were kissing her mother's head and the children stood around it in prayers for their late mother's salvation and for her soul being in rest in heaven. They expected their mother's soul will be accepted in heaven by the power of divine grace.

Cornelia started going school again. She had to recoup her lost work at school. She started working hard again.

Lazar seemed totally absorbed in his fishing in the sea. He got very good catch at times. He toiled day and night for the upbringing of his five little ones in a satisfactory way.

There lived a very pious woman named Agnes, next door.

She used to visit Cornelia and the children when they were at home and had friendly talk and sometimes helped Cornelia in the kitchen.

Agnes was a lonely woman in her forties. Her husband died in the sea years ago while catching a big fish. The fish drew him away on to the great vastness of the sea never ever to return to the land to see his lone wife sitting ashore day and night weeping for him.

After the sudden demise of her loving husband she worked as a doula to the coastal women of Anjengo for her livelihood.

Cornelia loved the lonely woman and she too loved the five as her own children and looked after the youngest two in the absence of the others at home.

Mary and Lily were washed, fed, and put to sleep. She often helped Cornelia in the kitchen, but never shared their food.

She cooked her own food at home and ate in front of her lost husband's photograph by asking him about his life in the heaven; whether he was happy there; when he was going to take her too to him and so on or so forth. She did not like anybody else's presence at that time.

The little angels, Mary and Lily took Agnes as a mother-figure to them.

Lazar was very much satisfied with Cornelia's progress in School.

But he was very much worried about the future of his two sons, Alex and Joseph.

They were very weak in their performance at school.

They used to skip class and loiter on the sea shore and pick fish from the boats and sell them to earn money to eat food from Prakassi's tea shop.

One day Father John, the headmaster of St. Joseph's Boys' school of Anjengo sent word to Lazar to meet him in the school office at once.

Lazar called on the headmaster after school hours. He stood in front of him in awe and respect.

The headmaster's kindly bearing caused everyone in Anjengo love and respect him.

The priest used a softly-softly approach with Lazar.

"Your sons are very weak in their studies, Lazar. They absent themselves in the class on almost all days. I can't tolerate children's absenteeism.

They are very good boys in their behaviour, character and conduct. But what's the use? They hate schooling and play truant. Could you, please, knock some sense into them?

Lazar, I heard your daughter, Cornelia is a genius and why don't you tell her to help her brothers.

Anyway I called you here to give you a warning."

Lazar went weak at the knees. He wore his heart on his sleeve and with a yearning look in his eyes he said, "I'll tell them, father. I have great expectations of my sons. I wish that they would at least get a pass certificate, a fifth form pass certificate so that they would get admission in the army. I want my sons to be good soldiers serving the country instead of going fishing in the rough sea.

Would you mind, father, giving them a chance to mend their ways?"

"All right, Lazar. You may go now and I'll try again to advise them not to bunk school for roaming on the sea shore or for skipping stones across the backwater. If I see them disobey my order, again I'll dismiss them from school.

"Thank you, father. May Jesus be with you, Amen." Wished Lazar and left.

Lazar reached home with a heavy heart.

He wanted them to get at least primary education to serve in the military. He wished his sons to be a part of British Military Service.

Lazar could smell beef curry when he entered the house.

He swallowed Saliva at the thought of Cornelia's special.

"The kitchen's smelt of beef curry. Where did you get beef at this time, Corne?" asked Lazar feeling very hungry.

"Miley's mother sent a pound of beef to us, father. There was a function there.

Miley told me that they are celebrating the death anniversary of her great grandpa.

Lazar enjoyed a delicious supper and went inside to have a short sleep till Alex and Joseph return from their daily loitering in the street outside.

At night Lazar thought of having his heavy cross to bear.

He called his sons to him and asked them to squat on the floor beside him.

Lazar's tone of calling them and his serious face made them squirm to think how badly their father had been interviewed by their headmaster.

"Sons, I have great expectations of you. You're my only sons. When you grow up it's your bounden duty to look after your three sisters. You know, my sons, there's no guarantee for my life. I fight with the sea to feed you. I know very well that I can't afford to give you a square meal eventhough I try my level best. You look as though you hadn't had a square meal for weeks. I feel sorry. But what can your father do? So if you have any love left in your heart for your father, please promise me that you'll attend the class regularly and study your lessons well until you pass your fifth form. You know, sons nobody's going to hand you success on a plate. You have to work hard to attain it.

Alex and Joseph look at each other for a moment.

They told their father that they could not understand anything in the class due to hunger and fatigue. Moreover they hated schooling and wished to go fishing when they grew up. At present they thought of fishing in the backwater.

Lazar got very hot under the collar and at last allowed them stop going school.

If they did not wish to study, what was the use of forcing them, was the policy of Lazar. He thought that every cloud has a silver lining.

So Lazar began to give them training in the backwater fishing. He taught them how to spread net, how to drag the net and other simple science of fishing. With a talent like them, the sky's the limit.

So instead of books, pencils and slates, they carried fishing nets, rods, hooks and lines.

They went angling with a lot of enthusiasm and a little bit of antagonism towards the school-going boys who used to mock them, "like father, like sons," They hated those boys and the teachers who were passing by.

\* \* \* \* \* \* \*

# Chapter 5

# A Nice Little Earner

One afternoon Prakassi Akka visited Cornelia's new house. The cleanliness there pleased her and she praised Cornelia for keeping the house in order. In spite of her hard work at school she devoted herself to the task of keeping her house and raising a family.

"Corne, I came here to ask you for a help to me. Can you spare a little time in the morning to wash my clothes, sweep the yard and wash my kitchen utensils. I'll pay you well for your service.

You see, my dear. I'm too old to do things properly now-a-days. I'm nearing my end, child. No one's there to look after me if I fall ill. Only a half an hour job. You won't be late for school.

Cornelia accepted the job with a lot of gratitude.

She was in need of money.

The family was living below the level of subsistence then.

Cornelia started to work from the very next day onwards.

When Shama and Miley came to fetch her she was not in her house. She was in Prakassi's very busy with the washing and cleaning.

Alex informed Shama and Miley that his sister went to do chores in Prakassi's for a pittance.

They left the house in a hurry as they did not want to be late.

When Cornelia came back, she was told that her friends had left without waiting for her.

Cornelia got dressed quickly. She always kept her school dress under hard pillows to get them pressed as an iron was beyond her wildest dreams.

While she was running towards her school, a feeling of abandonment started creeping into her mind for the first time in her school life.

She rushed past the shops and houses and at last reached her school on time. She was able to join the assembly.

After the assembly Shama and Miley questioned her where she was when they called at her house.

Cornelia only smiled. She could not tell them where she was and what she was doing there. She was freed for the time being when their class teacher appeared before them and ordered them to go to their class.

But during recess they caught hold of Cornelia.

"Corne, we want to know where you were in the morning. Alex told us everything. You went to do chores in another's house like a servant. We can't tolerate that business of your's. Tell us everything." Both Shama and Miley cross examined her.

"I beg your pardon, friends," began Cornelia "I've got an eight anna job in Prakassi Akka's for cleaning and washing."

"Washing and cleaning in another's house? Shama got irritated.

"How horrible!" Miley got surprised and frowned at her.

"We barely have enough money to keep our body and soul together." You know, my father struggles hard to make both ends meet. He has been punching more and more holes in his belt to tighten it. Now he can scratch a living from my part time job.

Eight annas is a big sum for us to run our kitchen.

She was on the brink of crying her eyes out in utter grief.

Shama and Miley felt pity for her.

Shama began to sob.

"I, I don't allow you to work as a servant in another person's.

"But nothing doing Shama. Now my father's in trouble. It's a boon to me this job. My brothers stopped going to school due to hunger and fatigue. How can they attend to school and listen to subjects with their empty bellies.

My poor father has to feed six mouths. He dices with death in the sea for that. It's because of your noon meal that I'm getting on well. But my siblings are suffering from deprivation. Nowadays our sea mother is slowly being depleted of her treasure and we fishermen, women and children are becoming a hapless lot.

It's because of Lord Jesus's grace that I got this job now and I should keep this to earn my keep.

Please, my friends don't think that your Corne is doing a menial job. I'm doing a service to an old woman who once gave us shelter and accommodated us in her inner comfortable room, helped us a lot, tried to console us, looked after my sick mother without showing any disgust or hatred during those disastrous and dangerous days. She was sympathetic and empathized with us at that time.

My mother breathed her last in her comfortable divan.

I can't forget anything, my dears, the glittering shroud with which my mother's body was wrapped in was her precious gift to my late mother.

She's not an another person; she's my own grandmother. I go to help my grandma not Prakassi Akka. Imagine like that.

It's because of my poverty that I am going to receive money from her. Otherwise my service to her would be free of cost. I'd have worked for her without receiving anything from her.

She's an important person to me like your grandfather who had gifted us an abode to stay in comfortably. Both of them are munificent personalities."

Shama and Miley stood silent for some time, In fact they were held spellbound by her oratory.

Shama decided to do something, as Cornelia's menial job in another's house made her lethargic.

She did not go to her mother for tea and snacks than evening.

Instead she went upstairs to change her dress. She bolted the room from inside and lay down on the bed. She shed tears. She began to feel that she was unwell. Kamini, Shama's mother saw her behaving in a strange way. Her unusual behavior made her upset for a while.

Then she called Shama aloud to come down and have her tea. But there was no response from above.

Kamini repeated her calls and the servants came running towards the foot of the stairs.

Kamini went up the stairs to call Shama and knocked at the door very violently because she got angry at the behaviour of the girl.

Shama's naughty behaviour usually made her mother mad.

She stepped down the flight of stairs in a hurry and informed her father-in-law about her daughter's strange behavior frantically.

"Come and see the new drama of your dear granddaughter. She's the apple of your eye who had shut herself up in her room. She is in a bad mood. Your pretty little granddaughter closeted herself away in her room.

Would you mind, father, handling the case? She's driving me to distraction today."

Grandfather, with a smiling face followed his daughter-in-law to Shama's room.

Hearing the hard footsteps of her grandfather, Shama got up from bed and opened the door for him.

Grandpa examined her pulse and touched her forehead to feel fever.

Everything found normal.

They got relieved of their anxiety.

"But why's she on bed at this time of the day?"

Kamini expressed her concern and frowned at the smiling Shama.

Shama hugged her grandfather.

Feeling the warm tear drop on his chest, grandpa lifted her chin up and saw her shedding tears.

Grandpa turned to his daughter-in-law and said.

"Kamini, please leave us for a moment. She's grieving over something very important. Let me find it out."

"Okay, father. Please knock some sense into her.

You can only deal with her stubbornness. I'm going. When I saw her abnormality in her behaviour I have made an offer of one gold coin to my deity to get her out of all dangers."

Kamini left them and when she came downstairs, she saw the whole servants standing at the foot of the stairs panic stricken.

"Madam, what happened to our little one?" They got frightened and thought that something serious had happened to their little mistress who was very loving, caring and humane in nature.

"Nothing to worry. It's all her drama to force her grandpa to pander to her every whim. He often falls into her trap of trying him to do everything for her.

You go and do your work. Don't waste your time on trivialities."

They thanked God and went to their work.

Grandpa sat on a chair and asked Shama.

"Now tell me. What's troubling you?" Shama could get over her worry. She became resilient and described about her friend, Corenelia's Chores in Praskassi's in the morning.

"My bosom friend, Corne started doing a menial job at Prakassi's. She washes her dirty clothes, washing up in her sink and clean her compound.

She had to go there before dawn and do the work only for eight annas. I don't want to see my innocent friend in that pitiable state.

Grandpa, if you believe in our earlier birth, I say surely, that she was my own sister in my earlier birth. She was your grand daughter. I don't want her to be a slave anymore. I wonder, grandpa, if you could pay that eight annas everyday in order to redeem her from doing a menial job in another's house."

Grandfather thought deeply for awhile and then agreed to help Cornelia.

"Ask Lazar to meet me tomorrow. I'll do the necessary. Now you go to your mother and please her. Have your evening tea and snacks and get ready for your daily routine. Your mother might have offered another gold coin to her deity for seeing you in happiness and merriment."

Shama jumped in joy and embraced the old man and tried to lift him up in joy. She shouted 'hurrah'. And ran down the stairs like a butterfly.

She ran into her mother's room in joy and hugged her tightly.

"Oh, mother! My great mother! God gave us a lot of wealth. Why don't we share it with the poor. You offer gold coins to your deity for my health and happiness. Why don't you give those sovereigns to the poor to make me more happy and contented. There are a lot of poor and destitutes living around us, mother. The deities are becoming richer and richer by the precious offerings of land lords and businessmen." Shama asked her mother by looking meekly at her. Her mother let go of Shama and said, "Aa ha! There lies the point. Share it with your fish girl, Cornelia, then.

You see, Shama, Your father toils day and night in his hospital in a foreign country to feed you and me. You know that? The wealth here is your grandfather's. The luxury you enjoy here is your grandpa's. He gave good education to his two sons. If they want money for their family they must work hard to earn it. That's your grandpa's policy. He had ordered them to do hard work and earn true money for the betterment of their wives and children. One must run his family at this own expenses and not with the wealth of the ancestral property.

Your grandpa had already divided the property into two equal parts and got them registered in their names just after the demise of his wife, my mother-in-law. But the sons will get them only after grandpa's passing away. Till then we're not rich. We're poor. We have nothing to share with the people around us." Kamini went crimson while she was speaking so tensely. She sounded tense and angry.

"I know everything, mother. You please, don't worry. Grandpa promised me that he would help poor Cornelia. Think mother, if she were your daughter, would you like to see her plight? Would you like to hear about her menial job in another house for eight annas? Her condition really threw me, mother!" Shama began to cry.

Kamini was suddenly put into a bad mood.

She shouted at her daughter.

"I think I'd take you away from that school and send you to Bombay and put you in Gaya and Gauri's school.

Bombay's a cosmopolitan city, where no one has time to worry over the plight of the poor and destitutes. My twin Sister Visakha is very strict and brings you up in a well disciplined manner. Here, your dearest grandpa sides you in every stupidity. Here your fish girl would make your life perilous.

Are you a new born Budda to alleviate the sorrows and sufferings of the poor? Think that you're an ordinary human being; not a saviour.

Grandpa had given to that fisherman and his children land and building to stay. That property and money are his two sons' shares, you know?"

Saying that much Kamini retired to her room to have a little rest.

Shama followed her mother and cuddled her and kissed her.

"Oh mother! Keep your shirt on mother. I'm your only one daughter eh? You once told me that I was born to you only after praying and offering to your favourite deity. It's your deity only made me so humane, generous and kind. What should I do? I'm like that. I can't ever change my principles of life." Cooed Shama.

"Okay, Okay. At last I admit your victory over me.

Take that girl to below stairs tomorrow. Not to the main building. No. not below stairs; but to the converted barn."

Giving the instructions she let go of her body from Shama's hugging and lay down on the bed.

Shama told Kamini that grandfather had asked her to bring Lazar the next day to have an interview with him.

On hearing this Kamini gave her a warning that she should not bring him to the main building and told her about their custom. They still held untouchability, a social evil prevailed among Hindu social class may years ago.

"Don't let the house pollute by their entry into the house, No more money to spend on holy rituals for its sanctity. Beware of that Shama. I can't tolerate your unwanted social conscience."

Kamini then had a nap. Shama was rooted to the place for a while staring at her mother and murmured to her angrily.

"Good bye! Good riddance."

\* \* \* \* \* \* \*

# Chapter 6

# Bete Noire

According to Shama's instruction Lazar called on her grandfather the very next day.

Shama directed him to the converted barn.

Grandpa was invited to the barn to meet Lazar and talk to him.

Shama asked Lazar to sit on a bench there.

She told her servant to bring some banana chips and a cup of tea for the guest. But Kalyani had a long face and murmured with hatred.

"I treat that fisherman like dirt. Tea and chips go to hell." Shama, for Kalyani's luck did not hear the comment.

If she had heard what Kalyani had murmured, she would have been torn to pieces by Shama.

Lazar was sitting there with a glum look on his face when Shama's grandpa entered the room,

Lazar stood up in respect and greeted him.

"Good afternoon, Sir."

"Good afternoon, Lazar. Please take your seat. My grand daughter is very much worried abut your daughter's new job at Prakassi's.

She wanted me to help you. First of all you ask her to stop going there. She had a lot of work at home, she had to study her lessons and how can a twelve year old girl do everything together while other girls of her age enjoy life. Don't put all burden on her head.

This morning I went to the Catholic Syrian Bank to deposit an amount in Cornelia's name, but being a minor I made you as the custodian and you have to transact with the bank.

You may withdraw an amount tomorrow to buy a boat of your own and other accessories so that you can go fishing in the far sea and earn a lot.

From your income you should deposit an amount a week in Cornelia's account. If you are not able to do that you may keep the necessary amount for a month in your custody and deposit it every month. That option is left to you Lazar.

You must also show me your pass book on the 5th of every month for my perusal and I'll return the passbook to you after checking. When Cornelia grows up she could use the balance for her education.

Lazar, whatever I did for you is because of my grand daughter's request. She loves Cornelia like her own sister.

Now, here's the passbook and cheque book. Please accept them and keep them in safe custody. Go and do what I have told you to do. Buy a good boat and net and other accessories needed."

Lazar knelt down and kissed his feet. Grandfather lifted him up and put the important book and cheque in his palm.

"Work hard, Lazar. You won't be able to make an omelette without breaking eggs. You can achieve success in life by the sweat of your brow. May God bless you, Lazar; to live in clover." Grandpa's words made Lazar to get spirited and he said,

"I have no words to express my gratitude. May Jesus bless me to pave a way to earn more and more money to pay the amount back. You spent a lot on my family and me. Only thing I can do now is to pray for you and your family, Sir."

Tears of gratitude and an implicit expression of his innermost feelings of satisfaction flowed down from his eyes.

Lazar went home and told everything to Cornelia. His heart was full of energy and enthusiasm and the new spirit in him forced him to achieve all through his hard work and deed of covenant.

Hearing about the great help Cornelia stood motionless for a moment. Shama had been helping her in many ways. How could she pay back for all these favours received from that angel.

She prayed to Jesus and Mary by kneeling down in front of their picture and kissing the crucifix.

Alex asked the children to wash their body and come for prayer. They all prayed for their benign and good-hearted guardian. They prayed sincerely for Shama's long life and grandpa's health and longevity.

Lazar asked Cornelia to stop her work in Prakassi's. She felt very sad for the bereft woman and she was put between the devil and the deep sea.

The poor old woman had no one to come to her. She found no one to trust. The only one man, whom She had trusted was Lazar.

No other person in the locality was allowed to enter her house because she was once robbed blind by a painter. So she did not like to make a rod for her own back Cornelia asked Alex.

"Alex, what should I do now? The relationship with her is something more than the money, dear. We have a moral obligation to help her.

Cornelia sat worried with her hands holding her head.

Alex thought for some time. At last he took it into his head to work for Prakassi in Cornelia's absence.

He declared that he could fill Cornelia's shoes.

"Alex, you're a child, not an adult to wash clothes and do the cleaning work. Her sink would be full of last night's washing up. You feel the work very tedious and difficult to handle. You'd be sick. I'm so dead set against your idea.

She tried a lot to discourage him.

Alex declared,

"There's nothing impossible for Alex in this world, my sister. Only washing and cleaning. Look at my strong palm with hard veins. I can do the work perfectly and our Akka will be pleased with me so that she will pay me more. The daily wage of eight annas will be a boon to us at this time to run our kitchen smoothly.

"Shut up Alex! You're doing my head in."

But Joseph also agreed to go with Alex and Lazar gave them permission to work there and make Prakassi happy.

They were as keen as mustard.

After a month's search Lazar could buy a boat in good condition with all paraphernalia for fishing in the far sea. The boat was in good condition and the fishermen in Anjengo came to have a look at it and agreed in one voice that the dealing was not a failure.

He appointed some very active and honourable workers to accompany him to the far sea for fighting with the angry waves for their livelihood.

The Vicar of St. Peter's Church and other priests of the area came and blessed his boat.

A small function was arranged on the sea-shore.

Shama's grandfather visited him and showered his blessings upon him.

The first day of the fishermen's venture in the sea arrived.

A crowd was there to see Lazar and his workers off to the sea.

The priests solemnized the inauguration,.

Men, women and children prayed for their lives when Lazar and his men slowly pushed the boat into the sea from the shore.

Lazar's five children, Agnes, and Prakassi knelt down on the sand and prayed for their safe return.

After the fishermen's departure Cornelia welcomed Prakassi to have a cup of tea in her house. But she rejected with thanks saying that she had to serve the customers waiting in her coffee shop.

"I'm well-pleased Corne! You're lucky to get a boat of your own. May Holy Mother bless you more and more because you're a good girl with fine loving character. I love you as my grand daughter and often visit me to make me happy."

She stroke her cheek with affection.

"Oh, Akka, We're always ready at your beck and call. Alex and Joseph will help you. They'll give you company. They love you a lot. Would you send word if you need any urgent help from me? I'll run to you. My father and I are always ready to look after you in your old age. We'll readily bring you here and take care of you as our grandmother." Prakassi went home satisfied.

Among the newly appointed workers there was a doughty young fellow, a dark horse.

Lazar loved him more than he loved anybody else in the team because he was an orphan.

He was a native of Quilon sea-shore.

He was a strong youth who could fight with the mad waves at sea and the boat was always under his stubborn control.

As he had no house of his own to stay he was allowed to stay with Lazar. Poor, innocent Lazar did not know that he was a snake in the grass.

Lazar's sons and Cornelia objected and they were against Lazar's decision of allowing him stay in their loving house. They did not want a stranger use their bedrooms. Moreover they hated the man's guts.

But Lazar called the children beside him and said with a pity.

"See my children, he's an orphan; he has no father, mother and no relatives.

He's a great help to me in fishing and drying the fish. He's an able man. He mends torn nets and repairs and maintains our fishing boat in good condition.

Other workmen do service only for money. But Peter's different. He takes an active part in the sale of both fresh fish and dried fish. We get good profit now-a-days. Shama's grandpa is very much pleased with my performance.

If Peter's with me I can earn more and deposit a portion inCorne's account every month.

So think well before coming to a decision. Be patient and show leniency towards that poor boy.

This house is not our's. This's an alm house granted to us by a caring and humane man of greatness. So allow him also to share the house and treat him as your elder brother."

Even though the children said nothing, Cornelia hated him for his nasty gestures and a sort of wicked smile in the absence of others in the house.

He, at times snapped his fingers to attract her attention.

One day, while no one was in the house, he even exposed himself to Cornelia. She always tried her best to keep him at a distance.

He was not allowed to talk to her while Agnes was in the house. Cornelia did not respond to his request for a burning splinter to light his cigar.

Agnes too hated the fellow and hauled him over the coals.

Cornelia had been warned to beware of him and to keep tabs on him when Cornelia informed her about the man's showing of his genitals to her.

Lazar's huge catch brought him fortune. He could deposit a good amount in Cornelia's account.

Grandpa praised him when he submitted the pass book for going through it. Lazar bought an umbrella for Cornelia.

The well paid workers of Lazar showed their sincerity and commitment to their duty and they tried even to fish in the far away sea.

The pay and bonus gave them new spirit and with renewed vigour they worked hard for Lazar.

Days passed.

The annual examination was fast approaching. Cornelia threw herself heart and soul into her studies. She wanted to come first in all subjects. So she burned the midnight oil.

Agnes proposed that Cornelia should join the stitching and embroidery class on all Saturdays from nine in the morning to half past twelve in the afternoon. Cornelia was given admission free of charge and she was the youngest trainee there.

One morning while Cornelia was doing her Maths homework with full concentration, she felt a soft pinch on the back of her neck. She jumped up like a startled rabbit.

Agnes and children were on their way to the church.

Alex and Joseph went to Prakassi's. Lazar and his workers left for sea before dawn.

Then who was there to pinch her. She had an intuition that something awful was about to happen.

Suddenly she recalled what Lazar had told her to do before he left home,

"Listen, Corne. Peter's ill. He needs some rest because he's suffering from severe back pain and he has a slight fever. He's sleeping inside. Give him some hot pepper coffee before you leave for school, Tell Alex to serve him rice gruel in the afternoon with a little lime pickle."

"Oh, the devil was inside." She thought. She had forgotten about everything because she was fully engaged in her studies only.

"I didn't prepare your pepper coffee. I've no time to do it. Let Agnes Aunty come. I'm in a hurry to go to school". Saying that Cornelia collected her books and moved towards her room to put on her school dress.

"Before coffee, I want to taste you. I've been mad about sucking your juicy lips. That'll be the best medicine for my false back pain. Come on, Corne. You're so beautiful. Let's make love.

In all probability he failed to understand the consequences of his action.

Catastrophe never waits for wise thinking.

He caught hold of the girl in a split second. His body was solid and taut.

Cornelia screamed her heart and soul out and struggled like a wild cat to get out of his strong hold.

Her scream was so loud that even Lazar in the mid sea felt an unknown shiver down his spine.

Lazar had a sense of forbidding that something worse had happened at home.

His heart missed a beat.

He informed his fellowmen that he needed some rest. He was rubbing his chest in pain.

The workers immediately spread some cotton sacks on the floor of the boat and helped Lazar lie down.

They gently pressed his chest and using a wet towel they wiped off his profuse sweat.

"Something might have happened to my kids at home. I heard the distant wail of my Cornelia. I'm dying to know what'd happened there.

The workers began to laugh and told him that they too had heard a distant wail of the wind as a harbinger of the oncoming storm.

A worker commented

"Leader, I too heard the wailing of the waves as if they thought that they were going to be clutched by the strong, dark clouds.

On hearing this Lazar burst into peals of laughter.

"There's nothing to worry at home. The heavy-set Peter's there, Uncle" said Lazar's nephew Robert to soothe Lazar.

"Okay, friends, Let's leave it and come to our duty."

Lazar got up and went to pull the spread out net. They toiled and at last the result gave them complete satisfaction. The catch was successful. But they had to stop their work for fear of the rumblings of thunder and the rising up of the waves.

There in the house Cornelia was fighting vigorously to let go of her body from his hard clutches.

She landed a punch on his chin and thrust her sharp nails into his flesh and scratched wildly.

The man turned nasty and threw her down on the cot and jumped over her and began to press her down and tried to undress her.

While his body was pressing against hers, a terrible fear, anger and might increased her heart beat and that could get her adrenaline flowing and she fiercely raised her right foot up like a sportswoman and thundered his scrotum with all her force. The man at once detonated with a woof and fell back unconscious.

The freed, Cornelia ran out of the house and suddenly let out a screech.

The men and women working on the beach heard Cornelia's screech and dashed towards her.

Alex and Joseph was returning from their work. They too ran towards her like winds.

Agnes and children too heard Cornelia's wild cries and they too ran to her.

By and by the girl fell unconscious on the sand due to asphyxia.

Alex shook her body, called her many times to open her eyes. But she was not aware of anything around her.

Joseph was told to get a pot of water from the house. He came back with a pot of water and sprinkled it on her face.

She opened her eyes and looked in fright at everyone's face that was watching her anxiously and with fear.

Joseph went home again to question Peter about what had happened to his sister.

But he saw Peter lying on the floor wriggling with pain.

Joseph thought that he was ill and was suffering from his bad back pain.

He felt pity for him.

"The poor fellow's writhing around on the floor in agony". Joseph told the mob.

The women helped Cornelia sit down. Agnes wiped her face and hands off sand and dirt.

"What'd happened to you my dear, in my absence?" asked Agnes softly in her ears.

But Cornelia began to shout.

"That wolf in sheep's clothing tried to molest me. I fought for my sanctity of life. Alex, Joseph thrash that nuisance out of our house."

Saying that much she fell down again unconscious.

The whole lot present there ran towards the house with sticks, oars, stones and what not and entered the room and inflicted severe punishment upon him.

The man was beaten and trampled to death.

The fishermen dragged his dead body along the beach and then it was hurled into the Arabian Sea who was gurgling with delight.

There ended the story of Peter. But there started an inner revolution in Cornelia's mind.

Shama and Miley came to fetch her to school as usual. But the sight of a crowd around the unconscious Cornelia made them run towards her.

They knelt down beside her and began to give first aid to get back her normal breathing. They lifted the girl and took her to the house. Agnes helped them.

Shama asked the crowd to disperse and they left for their usual work when they found Cornelia safe and normal.

Cornelia's mental shock and physical strain turned her to be an introvert.

She always liked to have some kip. She had lost her interpersonal skills.

She idled the days away without having any food. She became scraggy and low-brow.

Sometimes Cornelia stood absolutely motionless and stared at her friends, father and her siblings.

She used to stare at her relatives as if they were strangers to her.

Her face looked strained and weary.

Sometimes her brothers and sisters could hear strangled cries from her room. She gave a strangulated squawk. She relived the horror of the rape attempt every night in her dreams.

She was not in a position to attend her school.

The Staff and students of the school visited her and forced her to restart her studies. They made many attempts to bring her to normal.

The shock left her feeling listless and depressed.

The children of the Sacred Heart prayed for her speedy recovery.

Shama and Miley visited her daily after their school work. They brought for her sweet smelling flowers and fruits.

They tried their very best to take her out of herself and made her listen to the daily lessons, to their jokes or to the mock running commentary of sister Mercy Fernandus on the annual sports' meet at school.

Miley sang Cornelia's favourite songs to liven her up.

Shama began to wax lyrical about her new filigree ear rings.

But there was no response from Cornelia. She sat in front of them like a stone statue.

"Nothing but a miracle can cure her now". They said with extreme disappointment.

Alex, Joseph, Mary and Lily stayed near her and helped her in changing her clothes cleaning her teeth and face, combing her hair and tying them with a ribbon. Agnes fed her and took her to her room. But she did not sleep at all. She stayed in bed looking at the ceiling without moving her eyelids.

Lazar was in tears and prayed for her recovery from such a dangerous mental shock.

The little ones wished for her motherly affection which they were getting lavishly from her after the death of their own mother. She was not only their elder sister but also was their loving mother.

Shama's grandfather advised Lazar to take her to a psychiatrist in Trivandrum.

He made arrangement for their journey too.

Lazar requested Agnes to take care of his children in his absence.

Agnes agreed that she would hold the fort for them and blessed their journey.

All people of Anjengo prayed for the girl.

Lazar and Cornelia went to Trivandrum by a night service boat. They reached the city at dawn.

Cornelia was admitted in the hospital. The doctor examined her thoroughly and asked Lazar to admit Cornelia there for a month's treatment.

Lazar found it a hot potato and informed the doctor about his sea life and his fellow workers poverty if they stayed away from work.

"If they can't go to the sea they won't get anything to feed their family and children. They all depend on me, doctor. What should I do now. I want my daughter back as a normal human being I'm in hot water now."

The doctor felt pity for the poor innocent fisherman.

"I admit your difficulties, Lazar. But a by-stander is a must for the patient.

Not only that, the by-stander must be a loving, caring and a very intelligent person. Can you please arrange one like that?

Lazar thought of getting Agnes as Cornelia's by-stander. But what about the children at home. He was put between the devil and the deep sea.

At last Lazar could find a way in solving the problem.

Alex and Joseph were ordered to stay home and look after their young ones. They were not allowed to continue their work at Prakassi's till Cornelia return from the hospital.

Agnes came to the hospital to look after Cornelia.

The doctor's medication had no effect on the girl. There found no improvement in her condition even after a month's treatment.

She always sat in silence.

She had forgotten to smile. She lay down on the sofa looking out through the windows, sometimes crying, sometimes shivering with fear.

She had had a sense of impending doom.

The doctor allowed Lazar to take her home. He asked them to continue the treatment at home also and to arrange everything around her time-table and care her with a lot of love and affection.

"I think she may come to her normalcy in mind within a few weeks. Let's hope for the best and pray to God.

Shama and Miley wrote their annual examination.

They visited Cornelia after their examination.

She was having a cat nap at that time.

Shama gave her a soft slap on the back to make her get up.

The little Lily began to chat away nineteen to the dozen.

Lazar was spreading fish on the sand for drying when he heard the clapping and laughter from inside his house.

He came home running to see what had happened there. He saw his daughter talking to Shama about her old dream.

Shama and Miley hugged Cornelia and the children danced around the bed humming a folk song. Agnes too joined in their merry-making.

Lazar suddenly became very tearful.

'How're you now my child?" asked Lazar by holding her chin up and looking deep into her wide blue eyes.

"I'm fine, father. Thank you." She responded.

She got down from the sofa and the three friends walked to the inner bedroom and closeted themselves.

\* \* \* \* \* \* \*

# CHAPTER 7
# HOLIDAYS

One and a half months passed since Cornelia had fallen ill. On a Sunday afternoon one of the nuns, sister Philomina, the physical Education teacher of the Sacred Heart's visited Cornelia.

On seeing the teacher Cornelia tried to get up from bed and greeted the nun warmly.

Sister Philo smiled at her and she smiled back.

Sister Philo took her to the bathing place, changed her dress, cleaned and sponged her body with a clean towel. Agnes took out a new set of dress and helped Cornelia to put on.

She was given a glass of smoothie to drink. Sister Philo asked Cornelia to follow her to her school.

The headmistress had been waiting for them at the gate of the school and was eagerly looking whether they were coming or not. At last she heaved a sigh of relief when she spotted Cornelia and Sister Philo appeared in the main road.

They reached the gate.

The headmistress moved towards Cornelia and caressed her cheeks with a lot of love and sympathy.

"A good news, Cornelia. You've been promoted to sixth form after counting your high scores in the first and second terminal examinations.

The board of directors as well as the department head seconded my recommendation on your promotion and the government authorities gave me sanction to promote you.

Our school will begin to work after two weeks. Be a smart girl and fill your mind with good spirits and try to be dare enough to face the harsh realities of life.

You should come with your head high and sit with your friends in sixth form A division on the reopening day.

Cornelia thanked her headmistress.

Sister Philo then took her to the convent to meet the Mother Superior and other sisters there.

All inmates of the convent acted as if they knew nothing of the incident. They congratulated her for winning a gold medal as a good athlete from the Saint Joseph's Athletic Club of Anjengo. It was a surprise news for her. She took part in the January Sports Meet of the Club but she forgot about that and she did not know whether she had won the running race, pole vault or any other track events,

Cornelia was presented with the medal by Mother Superior as she was not in a state of mind to receive it from the school Inspector during the presentation ceremony held in the second week of March. The club kept the medal in the custody of the school authorities to present it to her later when she recovered from her illness.

Cornelia received the medal from Mother superior with a lot of thanks to her as well as to the Club.

Sister Philomina took Cornelia back to her house.

Lazar was in the house at that time. The sister told Lazar to take Cornelia to an English doctor in Madras whom she knew as the best counsellor of teens and a successful psychiatrist. Sister Philomina knew him personally and he loved Indians who were living below poverty line and treated them free of charge.

"I'll give you a letter, Lazar. Take her there and she'll be all right within a week. I'm confident that he will be able to cure her".

Lazar looked perplexed for a moment.

"You know, Sister, my limitations. I'm a poor fisherman, I'm illiterate too. How can I go to Madras to consult a doctor. I can communicate with him through my mother tongue only. Not only that Sister, Cornelia is slowly coming to her normal mental stage. She attends to her brothers and sisters and doing house chores. The other day she bathed her youngest sister and fed her".

Sister Philomina prayed for the family and said goodbye and left for the convent.

At the time of leaving she reminded Cornelia to begin attending the embroidery class so that she could fix her mind in one particular thing and slowly she could get over her shock and fear.

Sister Philo presented her with a rosary and entreated her to pray a lot.

After Sister Philo's departure Lazar told his daughter to be active and cheerful.

"I want you to be the same smart little butterfly as you were months ago.

See my sweet child you've a lot of responsibility to help moulding your siblings. You are in the place of your late mother.

Don't brood over the past events. Fill your mind with positive thoughts. You're a girl of many talents. Always think that God's blessings are with you. Get rid of your pessimistic view of life. Think about your future, Corne, and the future of your younger ones. They are yearning for your betterment. Get on with your hard work and dogged perseverance.

Cornelia rested her head on her father's chest and began to sob.

"My loving father, I try my level best to forget that spine chilling horror incident. But my head spins whenever I look at that cot and the way the wolf attacked me. Anyway I pray to my Holy Mother and Jesus to give me strength to overcome my present condition. Give me a little more time to make my heart and soul come in a line with my mind and body.

Father, here's my gold medal for winning the sports competition. You, please, keep this priceless treasure in your money chest".

Cornelia's gold medal had attracted the children. They gazed at the small round gold object and passed it over to one another to touch it.

Lazar left the house to have a bath in the backwater.

Cornelia sat down on a stool and began to write two post cards; one for Shama and the other for Miley.

Shama was taken to Bombay by her uncle Shiva and aunt Visakha to spend her vacation with their two daughters Gaya and Gauri.

Miley went to Ooty with her brother Lorrence to spend her holidays in her grandparents house.

Both Shama and Miley used to communicate with Cornelia through letters and post cards. They used to send to her beautiful pictures and photographs of important places. Cornelia kept them as treasures in her school box.

Uncle Shiva and aunt Visakha were working as doctors in a famous hospital in Bombay.

Their daughters Gaya and Gauri were studying in Dadar English School. Both were reputed for their academic excellence.

Gaya and Shama were of the same age. Gauri's was only seven and she was in second form.

Her holidays with her cousins gave Shama a lot of enjoyment, pleasure and happiness. They went frolicking on the beach. They visited gardens and caves.

Shama was taken to see almost all important places in Bombay. She could enjoy hearing the songs of Latha Mangeshkar and Mohamed Rafi.

The westerners' sun bath, the fishermen's strange attire, the special features of Hijadas with raspy voice and the busy people amazed her.

Often she went to the terrace of the house at night after Gaya and Gauri had retired to their room to sleep.

She enjoyed the Sight of the busy cosmopolitan city and the starry sky with millions of shining stars and a few silent planets. She wished if Corne and Miley were there on either side of her in those pleasant moments!

Then a sudden thought pricked her mind and she began to think about the present mental condition of her bosom friend.

She began to imagine that horror stricken nightmare of Cornelia. She thought with fright that if she were in the place of Cornelia she might have been killed by that rogue in his rape attempt. Cornelia could rip through him like a bullet and save her life because of her physical fitness and moral fibre. Her strong body and mind was the fruit of her domestic chores and her growing involvement with sports and games. Three cheers for my 'corne!

Shama got a postcard from Cornelia after a week. She wrote only six lines. But the card was a treasure to Shama. "I'm quite all right now, my friend. I started going to the embroidery class. The gold medal was presented to me by Mother Superior yesterday. I convey my great regards to your loving uncle, aunt, Gaya and Gauri. Pray for me and do write to me".

Shama felt satisfied with her friend's present condition and thanked God, for the favours received.

Shama gave Gaya the post card to read. She praised Cornelia's hand writing.

"Not only her hand but also her style of English is worth noticing. She speaks as well as writes English as if it were her mother tongue.

She's very beautiful and her physical appearance reminds us the painting depicting Lakshmi, our goddess of wealth. Shama was elated by the children's eagerness to hear more about Cornelia.

"Take her here with you during our next vacation. It'll be a great consolation to her. She'll be freed from her hard house work for at least a month, we can take her to visit many places in Bombay and make her thrilled at viewing the strange places and people. We too are longing to see your 'Lakshmi like' friend so that we can sprinkle flowers at her feet" Gaya said playfully.

"Oh don't pour scorn on my corne, please. She won't come. She's very duty-minded and loves her father, her brothers and sisters more' than the whole pleasures of the world. If I had had a brother of my own I'd have taken her home as my sister -inlaw. She's such a wonderful girl, a laburnum in blossom". Shama said with tears in her eyes.

"That's an impossible conditional clause, my cousin. She's a Christian. You're an orthodox Brahmin. No one would accede your wish. I beg to differ." Gaya said.

"If she's such an attractive girl ask any English boy there to marry her and take her to England. She speaks good English too. Anjengo is ruled by the English, isn't it? Gauri commented to Shama.

Shama burst out laughing. Gaya gave a hard pinch on her right ear and Gauri gave out a loud painful cry. "You're too small to crack such big comment. Don't be a big mouth".

"Shama, I have another idea to rescue her from her present embarrassing situation." Said Gaya seriously.

"What's that" asked Shama with interest.

"Let her be adopted by any English couple who are childless. When you go back to Anjengo search for a family without issue and request them to take her as their child.

They will surely give her good education in England. What do you say?"

"That's a good idea. Let me see. I'll ask for Lady Mary's advice."

They went to sleep after their serious discussion.

Next morning Shama got up from bed to hear a shocking news that her uncle Shiva was arrested by the British and was imprisoned for taking part in the freedom movement.

Visakha and children looked upset for a while but they returned to normality because they expected an arrest at any time ever since the Quit India Movement.

Uncle Shiva had been actively taking part in the freedom movement. In 1942 he was imprisoned for taking part in the Mass Movement under Mahathmaji's leadership.

It was only Shiva in Grandpa's family who took part in the fight against the British. Other members of the family were ardent supporters of the British. So they could enjoy good positions under their rule. They received better education from England.

Almost all of them often visited the country to carry out researches in various fields.

Grandpa had very close relationship with the British rulers and high officials. He made full use of this to influence the government to release Shiva from the prison in 1942.

Eventhough Shiva was emancipated, his spirit of patriotism and sacrifice was incredible and no one could change his decision to fight against the British for the freedom of his motherland. The British government arrested him again accusing him of conspiring against the rulers and sent to Dhulia Jail.

Grandpa was disgusted with his involvement in the freedom struggle.

His advice was turned down and Shiva even hated his father for favouring the foreigners.

It was on May 16, 1945 that Shiva was again arrested and sent to jail. He was a true Gandhian. He followed the ideas of Gandhiji. Before leaving home he asked his wife and children to go to Anjengo along with Shama to avoid the present grisly circumstances in Bombay.

So on May 20 Visakha and children got on the train to Trivandrum at Victoria Terminus.

Grandfather went to Trivandrum railway station by a car to receive his youngest son's family and Shama.

Grandfather did not ask anything about his son who was in jail.

But he was considerate towards his daughter-in-law and children. He put a consoling arm around their shoulders.

Gaya and Gauri found it very difficult to put up with the strange atmosphere in their ancestral home. Untouchability was prevalent among the inmates. The people's meticulous care regarding the cleanliness of the house and some set rules about what they should eat, how they should mingle with the people in and around the house and so on and so forth were driving them mad.

They hated the place and the tough nature of Shama's mother and the servants in the house. But Shama was a great consolation to Gaya and Gauri when they felt like fish out of water.

To make the situation worse there came a letter from Shiva from jail ordering Visakha to admit Gaya and Gauri in a Malayalam Medium School because he hated the English and their schools. Grandpa was at his wits' end. He called Visakha and asked her angrily. "How can they learn in a Malayalam Medium School without knowing the alphabet of the language, without knowing how to speak and write that language?"

"Please don't worry about that father. We can't send them to a Malayalam Medium School. Instead we can appoint a governess for the time being and let them continue their education here in the house.

Grandpa was satisfied with her wise decision.

After a long search for a governess, they found an Anglo Indian widow in Goa to be suitable for Gaya and Gauri. A new out-house was built on the western side of the main building. It was fully furnished and the lady was invited to occupy the house.".

Gaya and Gauri were very happy and contented to see a spiffy lady and they attended her classes with interest and they praised their teacher's natural aptitude for teaching children of high academic standard. Her commitment to providing quality education to the children was highly praiseworthy. Visakha was ordered to start a nursing home in Anjengo for the sake of the poor fishermen, women and children.

"You're a doctor. You continue your practice here. Instead of idling the days away, talking and sleeping, you offer your service as a doctor. I'll arrange everything for you to run a nursing home successfully.

Visakha was thrilled to bits.

Before long she started the nursing home for the poor coastal people.

Her service and medicines were free of charge. Patients thronged the nursing home. So Visakha had to toil a lot to examine each one carefully. She never sent away any patient dissatisfied or non-attended.

One day Lazar came to the nursing home with a fit of coughing. Visakha examined him thoroughly and advised him to take rest for a week.

He was given a bottle of cough syrup and asked him to take a spoonful three times a day after meals. She also told him not to take bath in the muddy river water.

"How's your daughter? Is she quite all right now. I want to see her. You better ask her to come to me tomorrow morning. I heard everything about her from my niece, Shama." Visakha enquired about Cornelia's present condition kindly.

Lazar informed the doctor that his daughter was not hundred percent recovered from her mental shock. She was an active, alert and skilled girl before that attack on her. At present she looked very weak and she was afraid of young men and sometimes broods over what had happened on that ill-fated day.

"Her school was re-opened and she said that she did not want to face the students there. Sometimes that would reopen the old wounds. She didn't have the courage to face her class mates." Lazar told the doctor with tears in his eyes.

"Okay, Lazar. Bring her here tomorrow morning. Let me check up. Lazar went home and told Cornelia to meet the doctor next morning. "Okay, father. I too wish to see Shama's Bombay doctor aunt.

Cornelia reached the nursing home before the patients had arrived.

Visakha was in the Office.

Cornelia was standing behind the half opened door. The mild knock on the door made Visakha turn her head back.

"Yes, Come in please." The doctor gave her permission to enter.

Cornelia approached the doctor meekly and with full respect.

Visakha's eyes glinted with happiness. She observed the girl and made a comment.

"Oh, you're Shama's goddess Lakshmi in flesh and blood.

Cornelia gave Visakha a blissful smile.

"I'm Cornelia, Shama's friend, "said the jittery girl.

Visakha asked her to take her seat in front of her. Cornelia obeyed.

"How're you, Cornelia?"

"I'm fine, doctor. Thank you very much".

Visakha thought that the girl was not from the Anjengo fishing colony. But she seems to be from a royal family in Trivandrum.

Visakha said, "You're very beautiful". She praised Cornelia to increase her sense of self-worth. "Your beautiful face is covered with grime and sweat. Please go and wash your face and, come back."

Cornelia moved towards the wash basin. After washing her face she came back to the doctor and waited for the next instruction.

The doctor handed over to her a clean towel to sponge her face.

"Go and lie down on the sofa over there. I'll examine you to find out what's in your mind and I want to pull it out straight away," ordered the doctor with a false seriousness.

The doctor examined every inch of her body.

"I will try to elucidate what I think your problems are. Now hold your breath for a second and then slowly breathe, out."

Cornelia repeated doing this breathing exercise.

Cornelia looked at the stethoscope in wonder and she turned her eyes to the solitaire nose ring of the doctor. She thought that the doctor herself is a worthy jewel. "Now I'm going to open your heart.

Tell me, what's troubling you?"

Cornelia was allowed to get up and sit on the sofa. She looked at the doctor with meekness.

"Cornelia, You're quite all right.

Nothing happened to you, girl.

You escaped miraculously from a human barracuda. That's because of the grace of God. You had been given a particular boon to bolster your courage and self defense. You had been given a chance to know what's this cruel world is. There are hundreds of poor girls and even infants are sexually harassed by uncivilized drop-outs and drunkards and they were thrown into a state of utter disgrace and hardship. I had to treat many rape victims with mental shock who had buns in the ovens.

You might have heard about little innocents who are being snatched off from the laps of destitute mothers and are thrown away dead or half-dead after raping them cruelly.

No one could protect them or save them from the clutches of these cruel men of loose morals. When compared to their fate, your case is only a phantasm.

Don't be left in a fit of pique. Be bold enough to face the world with a renewed vigour and determination. We, women must take the bull by the horns".

Visakha paused for a moment and observed carefully the change in her face. Cornelia's lips quivered and then she started to cry.

The doctor patted Cornelia on her head and continued "I'll give you a tonic to make your mind and soul strong and to make you more courageous.

Next time when I see you, you'll be a smart and spirited girl who attends school, Study well and score higher in all subjects. A bright future awaits you, Cornelia. Don't waste your precious time on brooding over useless matters. Try your level best to achieve great success in your life. God is there to give you strength and your Jesus is always with you to lead you to success.

Now promise me that you'll go to school from today onwards. I'll send Shama there to take you to school. Get ready by nine o' clock; This is my order, Cornelia, and you have to obey me."

Cornelia knelt down at the doctor's feet and kissed her hands with love and respect. Doctor Mam, I do always keep your words in my heart:. I have no words to express my gratitude towards you. I'll become an able girl from this moment onwards. Your words of encouragement suddenly flowed freely to me and I'm ready to face everything and everyone".

Cornelia lost control and tears began to flow.

Doctor Visakha was flushed with success after her first counselling was over.

She gave Cornelia a bottle of tonic to minimize her anaemia and to make her physically and mentally fit.

That morning was a grand one for Shama and Miley. They got their friend back from her bad mental state. They found Cornelia in a jubilant mood.

Cornelia was no more a pale, moody and neglectful girl.

She persevered with her house work and school lessons.

Lazar and children thanked God and prayed for the betterment of Visakha's family. They could show their gratitude towards her only through praying for her.

They lit candles in front of the images of Lord Jesus and Holy\ Mother Mary and Knelt down to pray.

"Oh, Jesus. Oh, Mother Mary. Our prayers are answered. Our Cornelia is safe and well. Thank you for your favours."

The children sang hymns.

Alex's eleventh birthday was celebrated elegantly.

The previous day's catch afforded Lazar enough money to buy a birthday gift for Alex and things to make a rich food for his family.

Cornelia prepared nougat, cake, beef-stew and apple dumplings.

It was a marvelous day for Cornelia. She invited her friends Shama and Miley to share her enchantment. All were happy and thrilled at the pomp. Shama accepted a bowl of strawberries with lashings of cream, without demur she tasted it. She was eating out for the first time in her life.

* * * * * * *

# Chapter 8
# The Bread Vender of Anjengo

Lazar was worrying about his shortage of fund lately. He thought he had a heavy cross to bear.

His low income from his small catch of fish barely covered his expenses.

He could not deposit the prescribed amount in Cornelia's account that month. But grandfather allowed him to pay back in dribs and drabs, not all at once. Even then he felt that his debts were a millstone around his neck.

Fish stocks in the sea were in decline due to man-made calamities.

The sea was the fishermen's treasury from which they could withdraw a little to meet the needs of their family.

The sea was his mother always looked after him with huge catch of fish.

At present sea-mother seemed aggressive and showed restlessness, resulted in the reduction of her marine supplies.

She reduced the fishermen to tears.

"She'd like to wipe our tears by allowing us reap the benefits.

But she was not able to do this because of the depletion of fish stocks"

Cornelia wanted to help her father, So she started stitching frocks and petticoats for the school girls. The money she got from the work was deposited in her account to please Shama's grandfather.

The stitching work was found tedious as she did it with her hands.

A sewing machine was beyond the realms of possibility.

Now and then she watched Lady Mary sitting at her sewing machine operated by hand and stitching her dresses.

She wished she had not been born so poor, for the first time in her life.

Then she repented for her wild thoughts and begged Lord Jesus's pardon.

Alex thought of doing something to help his father. He put his thinking cap on. He thought of making some eatables and selling them among the folk and getting an income.

He shared his ideas with his elder sister and sought her advice.

Cornelia agreed to cook some food items early morning. Alex should take them in baskets and sell them among the people on the coast.

Alex became a healthy and hard-boned boy because of his backwater fishing.

He had a friend named Johnson who often came to help Alex in catching fresh water crabs and lobsters at night. He used lobster pots to trap them. He had a special knowledge of where the crabs could be seen and the particular holes in which they hid. He used a long arrow like metallic stick to pull the crabs out of their hiding places. He could bring home the bacon in catching big black lobsters and crabs. Alex and Johnson were on the same wavelength.

Johnson's father was a long-shore man in a distant port. He neglected his wife and children. So Johnson too was in need of a job and an income to support his poor mother and his divorced sister Veronica. Her husband and mother-in-law had kept her skivvying day and night. And so she took to her home and that led to a divorce.

Alex discussed the business with Johnson and invited him to join it.

"For the time being we can prepare pancakes to sell among our people. Those Travancoreans who come and sell their items among the sea side people drain our people's money away. We must tell our people to buy our items." Said Alex as if he were a skilled businessman.

"I think it is better to sell our items at a reduced price. That'll attract our customers." Said Johnson seriously.

Cornelia was handed over a little money that Johnson had in his pocket.

She took out her money-pot from the kitchen cupboard and broke it. Alex and Johnson picked up the coins which were found scattered on the floor.

Cornelia counted the money.

She was satisfied with the amount and sent Alex and Johnson to buy the necessary food items for preparing pan cakes and veggie burger.

Cornelia was a very capable cook.

She got up with the lark and prepared the items very carefully. She wanted her discriminating customers buy the items and ask the question.

"Who cooked this? It's delicious." Then there would be an increased demand for the items.

Cornelia's attractive packaging of the food items impressed Lazar and he sent the boys out with blessings for their first sale. Their first attempt turned out to be successful. They floated on air.

The people of that area liked to eat the items hot and found them more delicious and hygienic than those which the Travancoreans had brought for sale.

Alex and Johnson were very happy because the results exceeded their expectations.

Men, women and children from each and every shelter came out to buy their tasty food.

The little boys' first sale generated record profit.

Some poor women were allowed to pay later as they had no ready cash with them. The boys gave the full amount they had got out of the sale to Cornelia.

She was elated by the prospect of the new business ahead.

She divided the profit into two and gave Johnson one portion. But Johnson gave the amount back to Cornelia for the next day's purchase. He liked to prime the pump!

Cornelia forced Johnson to accept an amount as his wage for the service. But he politely refused to accept it.

Alex became the sole bread winner.

The children's business thrived and they could save a little of their own.

Shama and Miley came to know of Alex's pancake-burger business and they too deposited their pocket money in order to expand the eleven year old boy's small enterprise.

One day while Alex was fishing in the backwater near Shama's coconut shed, she spotted him. She was swinging on the lower bough of a guava tree.

"Hello, Alex. How're you?". Shama greeted him.

"I'm fine. Thank you my dear sister. "Alex smiled at her for a moment and then turned to his work.

"How about your breakfast business?" Shama asked in a serious tone.

"I think you're a boy of mettle and might. Keep it up Alex."

"That's very nice of you to pay me a compliment."

Alex was a boy of wit and intelligence. His eyes twinkled with amusement and said.

"One day I'll be a great merchant of Anjengo. Then you may call me the merchant of Anjengo.

Shama burst out laughing.

Her altruism was well known in Anjengo. "Now allow me to start fishing." Alex threw his net on the water and waited for the net to sink.

Shama watched him fishing.

Alex pulled the net towards him. He lifted the net and went to the shore to spread and see whether he had a good catch.

He found only a few minnows.

Alex repeated throwing the net and drawing it and spreading on the ground. He saw only some shrimps. He kept his collection in a basket woven from coconut leaves.

Alex gave Shama a warm glowing smile.

Shama got down from the guava bough and ran towards him. The shrimps were flopping around on the ground. Her eyes flicked from shrimp to shrimp.

Alex respected only two persons in Anjengo. One was Shama. The other was Father John.

Father John gave him lessons on all Sundays and taught him how to behave in society, how to lead a moral life and what all things he needed to make his life a success. He had been taught about religious faith and beliefs.

It was Father John who had helped his father a lot during their adversities.

Alex loved and respected the priest for his kind nature, good advice and perceptiveness.

Alex threw the net and waited.

This time when he dragged the net he found it extraordinarily heavy. Somehow or other he tried to pull it towards him.

He was amazed at the sight of a carp in his net.

Alex lifted the net with great difficulty and slowly crawled on to the bank to let the fish free from the net. It was fluttering and slithering to give Alex the slip.

Shama looked at the wonderful fish for a moment. Then she uttered a cry.

"Alex, please let the fish go to the water and breathe. How cruel it is to watch it die!"

Alex made fun of her.

"Don't be silly, please. This is my first big catch. I'm a fisherman's Son. I won't let my fish free.

Please, my dear sister, don't get worried over a catch. It's my source of livelihood." Alex told Shama calmly.

But Shama went crimson.

"How much do you get if you sell it, Alex?"

I'll give you the money. Please throw it into the water immediately. Let it live in its natural environment."

The fish stopped its movement and lay on the ground without life.

Shama gazed at the dead fish for a moment and then cringed in terror. "It's a crying shame to kill a living being." She thought.

Alex noticed her change.

"Look, Sister, even if I threw it back to the water, it would not live longer. If it lives, someone else will catch it. It's a biological law that fish must be caught by fishermen. Otherwise it'd breed and breed and the whole water in the river gets polluted. See, we men should die after living a certain period. Otherwise there'd be population explosion. It's our mother nature's law. The balance of Nature should not be upset.

Look, Sister, Father John taught me the other day about the ecological balance. He told me that flies are created by God for frogs and frogs are for snakes. Snakes must be eaten by hawks. This process of consumption is very necessary to balance our mother Nature.

A fisherman's duty is to catch fish and sell it for his daily bread and butter. Thereby he tries to balance his family. I'm doing my duty. The carp only helps me by getting itself trapped into my net."

Alex began to lift the big fish from the ground and tried to put it into his basket. But it was too big to go into it.

So Alex tied the fish by thrusting long woven spiky leaves through its gill cover and hung it up on his shoulder by holding the leaf end with his right hand. The dead fish lay on his back that made him stoop a little.

Shama stood like a stone statue for a while. She then made a comment.

"Your father John is a wise man. Thank you Alex. I learnt a lot from you. There's no use of attending school for scientific information and life ideals."

Alex doubted for a moment whether she was making fun of him. Neglecting the tone of the comment Alex replied smartly.

"Yes, of course. The priest is a very wise man. He's a fatherfigure to me. He's my all in all. I respect him because it is he who made me a literate boy even though I stopped schooling. You know, sister, school is not the only place to impart education. We can be knowledgeable about everything in this world under an all rounder like Father John."

Shama's tension began to melt and she expressed her willingness to accept Father John's theory of existence.

"I too wish to get environment lessons from Father John. But it's difficult to come to the church. My customs are invariable and strictly against yours."

"Don't worry. Whatever I learn from him will surely be imparted to you." Alex said to her with a hearty smile. "Now its time to leave. Good bye, Sister. Have a good day."

"Are you leaving now. Alex? No more fishing today?" Shama asked him surprisingly.

''I'm afraid, no I've got enough and more. I mustn't be greedy." Saying so Alex walked slowly away from her with the heavy fish on his back.

"Alex, mind out for the dogs." Shama warned him from behind.

He went to Miley's father to hand over the big fish for a good price.

"It's very kind of you, Alex, to take the fish here instead of to the market. You're very kind like your father, Lazar. Very hard working indeed! Keep it up my boy. May God bless you."

Alex gave the money and the little fish he had caught that day to Cornelia. She felt very happy and asked him to hand over the amount to father by giving back the amount to Alex.

Days and months passed. Alex could save a little each day. He kept his savings in a small money bag and kept the bag behind the idol of Jesus Christ on a stand. He wished to buy a new sewing machine for his loving sister Cornelia. But what Alex proposed was disposed by God.

His youngest sister Lily was stricken with pneumonia and Alex had to spend his savings to buy her costly medicines from Trivandrum.

Alex loved his brother Joseph and his three sisters and waS always ready to shoulder the responsibility for their upbringing. Lazar was proud of his eldest son who had much talent to make his siblings' lives successful.

Cornelia felt relieved a lot when Alex rose to the occasion.

Lazar went to the church, knelt down before crucifix and prayed. His eyes were raining when he murmured his prayers in gratitude for the blessings of Lord Jesus to give him such a good children like Cornelia, Alex, Joseph, Mary and Lily.

He prayed for the salvation of the spirit of his dear wife. She had done only good things while she was alive and so she might have gone to heaven.

\* \* \* \* \* \* \*

# Chapter 9

# A Woman Dripping with Gold

Anew family of seven members from the south of Trivandrum came and settled near Lazar's.

They belonged to a fishing community. Their slang had a slight Tamil touch. They were not rich but the women wore a lot of gold ornaments on their necks, hands and legs. They wore very big ear ornaments. Their nose rings had diamond studs. Their hair locks were adorned with fresh jasmine garlands.

Among them was a young woman of sweet seventeen. She was dripping with gold. She made waves.

Her dark long hair dripped down her back. She was a fair maiden. But she had a sharp tongue. She did not keep a civil tongue in her head to bad guys and immoral persons. She was a reckless daredevil.

She used to stand with arms akimbo and scold and curse those men who made very unfair cracks about her looks stunning and stylish, and her way of walking with her long plaited hair move to the swing of her hips.

No men ever dared to talk to her for fear that she might go ape shit and run amok if she didn't like their comments.

She sometimes went to the market to sell big fish like tuna, shark, trout and big prawns.

Men and Women came to her to buy her fish without much bargaining because she sold her items at a reasonable price. She even allowed the poor to pay her in dribs and drabs if they did not have enough money to pay all at once for the fish. She did not like anybody test the fish or pull them out from her basket.

She never sold any decaying or rotten stuff.

One day one of the tapioca merchants in the market, a Muslim approached her and took out a tuna from her basket without her permission.

He asked her its price. She answered that it cost ten rupees. Even though she did not like his behavior she kept quiet.

The man, holding the fish in his right hand he tried to take out ten rupees from his undergarment's inner pocket with his left hand. While doing this he purposefully exposed his genitals.

She was so furious that she could not control herself and punched him out in anger.

She snatched the fish from his hand and snarled abuse at him. A crowd soon gathered around them. The man went berserk and tried to catch hold of her. But the woman took out her machete and chopped off the fingers of his left hand. The man howled in pain and fell down unconscious.

There raised a hue and cry among the Muslim merchants. But she was rescued immediately and the police were informed to avoid any communal riot.

The woman was taken into custody and took her to the police station.

The wounded man was sent to a hospital along with his chopped off fingers in a polythene bag.

The women buyers and sellers in the market had given the woman lots of support and stated that what she did was a great thing that many had already wished to do. They hated the man for his notoriety in philandering and his cracking of vulgar jokes to their faces.

The police officer set up an enquiry into the chopping affair.

The woman in custody argued adamantly and claimed that she had done the right thing to save and protect her virginity.

"Those fingers of him were a misuse. I'm ready to face the repercussion. I'm unrepentant. He is the instigator of the happening."

The police officer was a soft hearted man. He had a daughter of her age.

He felt as if his daughter Soudamini were standing before him with the same batting eyelashes.

He asked the policemen about the character of the plaintiff. The inspector was informed that the tapioca merchant was a notorious womanizer and a full time drunkard used to tease women in the market. He was under the influence while dealing with the girl.

"You chopped off the man's fingers. He's in the hospital. How are you going compensate his loss. He has to undergo a surgery."

The woman did not answer the inspector. She stood in front of him like a stone statue.

The inspector got Irritated at her rebelliousness. "Ei, what's your name?" The inspector asked her angrily by beating his truncheon on the table.

"Emily Solomon." The girl murmured.

"Are you new to this place?"

"Yes, Sir.'

"Where d' you come from?"

"From Trivandrum South."

"Why d'you wear a lot of gold ornaments? You sell fish in the market, not a bride on her wedding day." The inspector asked her to remove the ornaments and keep them on the table.

"But it's our custom. I can't remove them."

The inspector beckoned the head constable and asked whether anybody from her family had come there to take her on bail.

Emily's parents were waiting outside crying. They were summoned in.

Her parents knelt down at the feet of the police officer and prayed for his mercy.

"Please pardon my innocent daughter, your highness. The man has been trying to insult her and prattling about her breast and bum ever since she came to the market to sell fish. She never in her life reacted without genuine reason. She did a brutal crime, we accept. But she did it only to protect her virginity and lady like nobility. If you pardon her, I'll take her to my native place and we all will leave the place." Emily's father entreated the officer with folded hands.

The officer felt for the man, He knew that she was the apple of her father's eye. "Do one thing, man. You go to the hospital and pay his hospital bill and pay him off to prevent further calamity. You stay in the hospital till he becomes normal. Otherwise your daughter, this deadpan will be sent to jail."

Emily's father admitted his verdict.

He took his wife aside and ordered her to sell or leave her ornaments with a pawnbroker to get enough money and send it, through Alex or Lazar to him immediately. The woman ran home.

It took an hour to get the money.

Lazar came to the office with the money. "You go to the hospital and look after the casualty. Let the girl be here." ordered the officer.

Lazar felt pity for the girl.

But she was stern.

The inspector thought the girl was made of sterner stuff "Is there no value for a woman's pride and privilege, Sir?" She asked the officer with her eyes raining.

The officer watched her cherry lips trembling. He became soft and asked Lazar to take her home.

The young women of Anjengo praised Emily for her act of valour and dare. They took up the cudgels on behalf of Emily.

They often faced unpleasant treatment of the fish merchants who visit the coast for buying fish in bulk.

Being poor and helpless they were unable to react against the fish merchants' intolerable behavior.

They did not want to inform their men for fear of a feud in the sea shore between the merchants and the fishermen.

So they had been bearing all sorts of misbehavior, sexist language, vulgar signals of the merchants for a long time.

Thus Emily became their super heroine and a modern warrior.

Emily stopped going to the market.

She joined the embroidery school and learnt stitching and embroidery.

Emily was a casual visitor of Cornelia and children.

One afternoon, when she went there, she saw Lazar laid up in bed with a high fever.

His body was shivering with high fever. She ran home to fetch her father's blanket.

She covered his hot body and gave him some hot ginger coffee to drink.

Lazar thanked her in a soft voice. The little Lily was sitting beside him and crying.

Don't cry baby, Your father's okay. His fever escapes from him with the potion I'm going to give him."

Emily went home to take some dry leaves kept in a pomander and crushed them fine and made a drink out of that. She forced Lazar to drink the bitter medicine.

She put wet pieces of cloth on his hot forehead to alleviate fever.

She kept a bowl full of cold water and wet clothes on a chair near Lazar and asked Lily to repeat the treatment till she came back. She went home to inform her father about Lazar's severe fever.

Emily's father immediately went to Dr. Visakha to get medicine for Lazar.

When Cornelia and Alex came home they saw that their father was feeling pretty bad and how Emily and her father's immediate attention on him made the situation less serious. They exchanged relieved glances and thanked them for their service to their sick father.

Lazar's health improved in leaps and bounds.

But his children did not allow him to go out of his house for a few days.

Lazar had a lot of feeling for Emily. For the first time after his marriage he felt his age. He was only thirty years of age. His father forced him to marry at the age of seventeen. At present he was a widower with five issues.

He thought of Emily the seventeen year old girl, who was strikingly good looking and good hearted. He was imbued with a desire for her being his bride. He began to love her from afar. He decided to bide his time until he got an opportunity to talk to her alone. He cudgeled his brain.

But soon he was able to distinguish between imagination and reality.

"How can a young girl be the wife of a thirty year old widower!" He said to himself and nipped his vile feeling in the bud.

Cornelia had a soft spot for Emily ever since they came and settled in Anjengo. She loved and respected her for her boldness, cherished way of approach, wisdom and beauty.

Alex used to visit her to hear her biblical stories and prayer songs.

On a Sunday morning Lazar met Emily on her way to the Church.

Emily asked joyfully.

"How're you, Lazar brother?"

Lazar answered very cheerfully.

"I'm fine. Thank you Emily."

"Please don't stop taking that medicine."

Emily advised him. "I love and respect you because you're a teetotaller like my loving father."

"Thanks for your compliment." Lazar said with a smile.

In order to continue the conversation Lazar asked her.

"What about that chopping case, Emily?"

It was an unexpected question.

Emily went crimson and shouted at Lazar.

"Ei, Lazar brother don't be over smart. I hate you ask such a dirty and devilish question. I thought you're a gentleman. Why don't you ask me something about the church service, my stitching lessons or about my welfare?

Lazar was perplexed by her response.

"I beg your pardon, Emily. I didn't mean to hurt you. Please bear with me.

But Emily disregarded his apology and turned and headed for home. She did not want to go to church in such an angry mood.

There was a lot of effing and blinding going on.

Lazar, for the first time in his life, felt guilty and humiliated.

The very next day Lazar called on Emily and requested her to pardon him. "Lazar brother, you're a respectable fisherman of Anjengo. All love you and your family very much. We're constantly at your beck and call when a situation arises. But mind it, you mustn't try to thrust a pin on somebody's ulcer."

Lazar felt ashamed of himself.

"I'm extremely sorry, Emily. I don't know why I asked you that question. Perhaps I was trying to continue our conversation. Any way my tongue cheated me. You know I'm not that type to tease women. Forgive me this time. I'll be careful here afterwards."

Saying this Lazar left her home.

Emily's mother scolded her a lot.

"So many are asking me the same question. Can you go and fight with them all? Why d'you blame the poor Lazar alone? Go and blame everyone in Anjengo, you reckless dare devil."

Emily dashed towards her mother. "Mumma mind your words. I did the correct thing. I might have chopped that guy's head off. I could not tolerate anyone's bad behavior towards me. Did I ever interfere with anyone's affairs in my life? If anyone tries to hurt my Christian morality, I'll not allow him or her to exist in this world.

Lazar heard her shouting from behind.

He remembered his demised wife's calmness, religious fervor and femininity.

He felt sad about his great loss and cried his eyes out on his, way home.

A month passed.

Lazar was talking with Father John in his retiring room after the mass about the coming Christmas festival.

In the middle of the conversation the priest informed Lazar that the Muslim merchant kept his nose clean after leaving the hospital. His surgery turned successful.

The Police officer tried his best to change him into a good Muslim.

Lazar felt relieved a lot and prayed for everyone's welfare.

He knelt in prayer for Emily.

"May Jesus be with her, guide her, let her lead a successful life. Oh, Lord no more police investigation. She should be given a verdict not guilty." Lazar prayed.

Lazar exchanged the news to Emily's father. But when Emily heard the news she spat on the ground, saying "Nefarious dog! How can a leopard change its spots?

It was December ten.

Emily was summoned to the office of the Police Inspector.

An amicable settlement was reached and the officer wanted to close the file without further legal proceedings against the young woman.

She appeared before the officer.

She was shocked by the man's presence in the office. He was standing in a corner with his head low in respect. The very sight of the man turned her a deadly shade of white.

The inspector called her to come near. She moved slowly towards him and stood there with her head high.

"Look here, D'you know this man?"

"Yes, your honour. I know him well." She answered by getting on her high horse.

Her tone aroused the officer's anger. But he controlled himself for a minute. "Mr. Jalaludhin had been summoned here to settle the case. He had been given compensation by your father for prising his fingers. But now I say you must apologize to him for your inhuman behavior."

Emily could feel anger boiling up inside her.

"Why should I apologize to this mean creature. He exposed his genitals in front of me. He tried to touch my hand while taking the fish out of my basket. My honour, I'm leading a life of virtue. I could not tolerate his molest attempt. That's why I chopped his fingers off. This sex-maniac made me do that."

The inspector, got so angry that, he got up from his seat and slapped the girl hard enough to make her head swirl and she fell unconscious on the floor.

A police constable was asked to sprinkle water on her face.

She opened her eyes.

Her father looked at her with pity and love and lifted her up to sit down.

"Who do you think, you are, fish girl. A good for nothing idiot. I'm going to send you to jail and be safely behind bars. You think you're the bee's knees?

I tried a lot to settle the case. Otherwise you would have been raped by the Muslim youths and split your body into pieces. It's your luck this gentleman kept his nose clean. You were done for, idiot, without his change.

Now I can't bear your disobedience." The officer sat down to write a report to the Magistrate.

Emily's father wailed in fear and knelt before the officer to give her a chance.

He turned his head to Emily and asked her to apologize to the man.

Mr. Jalaludhin needed no apology. But the officer was adamant that she must apologize.

"Emily, do what his highness ask you to do. It's all for your safety." Said Emily's father. She raised her eyebrows and asked, apologize? Why? Please father, hold no brief for that bad guy. Emily got up from the floor, ran out of the office and dashed off towards her sea-mother, the Arabian Sea. She called out to the sea, "Take me in your arms, sea mother. Please hold no brief for that scoundrel."

The turbulent sea welcomed her, embraced her with her high waves in an eerie elation.

\* \* \* \* \* \* \*

# Chapter 10
# The Gloomy Christmas

E mily Solomon's body was fished out of the sea by Lazar and his men.

Hundreds of people attended her funeral. The nuns, priests, the police, school children, Market people including Muslims stood in silent homage around her grave.

A special prayer meeting was arranged in the church yard after the funeral ceremony.

After that macabre incident the police officer, Mr. Ananda Sharma left his job and went to his native place in Madras. The people of Anjengo dropped the incident firmly back in his lap.

He, people say, led a pious life there, serving the poor and the destitutes.

Emily's parents and other members of the family left Anjengo. They went back to their native coastal village.

But the woman dripping with gold lives in the minds of the Anjengo people. Her memory lives on. The terrible scenes were indelibly imprinted on their minds. Their Christmas was gloomy.

The people, especially Lazar and family spent their days gloomily.

The Christmas in 1946 was not properly celebrated by the school children of the sacred Heart.

Even after the Christmas holidays Shama, Miley and Cornelia were not in a mood to attend their classes because it all sounded highly improbable about Emily Solomon, her tragic and untimely death.

There were unrest everywhere in the country at that time.

Young Christian men of Anjengo secretly assembled in various boat-sheds and in big fishing vessels to plot against the British Government and to make them quit their mother land.

News of people fighting everywhere to put the British to rout.

Many politicians welcomed arrests and were ready to be imprisoned for a very good cause, the freedom of their Nation.

The Travancoreans were in the front to fight. People in Anjengo were afraid to work against their rulers in the open. So they tried to stay out of the limelight.

National leaders in the capital were busy talking with the British authorities to settle the matter soon and give freedom to India.

A new Police officer was appointed in Anjengo in the place of Mr. Anand Sharma.

The new officer, Mr. John Brio, was an ardent supporter of the British rule. He trumpeted their achievements and hated those who were fighting against them.

He arrested many young men and were arraigned for freedom fight. His third degree method and bureaucratic procedures had been hated by the people wherever he was appointed as a police inspector.

So he had earned a nick name 'Blood-hound' and women used to escape from his sight as he was a philanderer.

In Anjengo he started to work by introducing himself to the important English personalities and high officials and to his subordinate officers and rich merchants of the place.

A month passed without any notable events.

Someone in Anjengo had informed him of Visakha's husband's jail term. He wished to see the young doctor who was running her nursing home in Anjengo even though her house was in Travancore.

John Brio visited the doctor to question about Shiva's involvement in freedom fight and his imprisonment. He had a good sniff around.

He used unparliamentary language.

Visakha seemed unperturbed by his way of questioning, She was a forceful personality who didn't suffer fools gladly. She sent her peon to call grandfather out.

Grandfather sent the man to the Magistrate's office with an urgent message to his nephew.

John Brio was continuing his questioning.

"I heard that you're also fighting against us along with your husband?"

"What d'you mean by 'Us'? Visakha answered by asking the question.

'Us' means the British."

"But you're an Indian not an English." Visakha nailed her colours to the mast.

"Every patriotic Indian should rise up against the British to make India free. This is our country. We are its owners, not the British. I'm one of Bharath Matha's daughters. "Be Bharathma Victorious." She shouted at him.

John Brio was burning with rage. His hands were stimulated to beat her. But he had to control himself as she was not only a doctor but also the daughter-in-law of a man of substance.

He stormed out of the room.

On his way he met an officer from the Court with a warrant for his arrest for his unnecessary intrusion into a lady doctor's cabin for unwanted questioning and also for usurping the power of higher authority.

John Brio was taken to the Court and he was suspended for a week.

After a week he joined his post. The first thing he did was, he went and apologized to Visakha and grandfather.

John Brio was welcomed in the out house. He was given due respect and they treated him to lunch. Thus John Brio became grandpa's family friend and was presented with bunches of bananas and other fruits from grandpa's garden.

He often took his wife and his only daughter Josephine to grandpa's for a friendly visit.

Shama saw Josephine in seventh B class, the newly admitted girl with long fair slender body, beautiful face with big eyes. She was an eyeful girl with a pleasing beauty spot. She had a dimple which appeared when she smiled. She was a trim figure.

Shama did not know, then, that she was the Police Inspector, John Brio's only one daughter.

Now they became friends.

The next day Shama introduced Josephine to Miley and Cornelia.

Moly Fernandes, the sweeper in Miley's house was a belle belonged to a very poor Anglo-Indian family in Quilon. Her father was a British through and through.

She and her mother came to Anjengo only six months ago in search of job in English people's bungalows. But they were not successful as many English families left Anjengo by that time.

Miley's mother accidentally met that girl on her way to church.

She asked her about her whereabouts and Moly was asked to sweep the house and yard for a small sum. She agreed immediately and from the very next day onwards she became a regular sweeper in Miley's house.

Moly's mother a young beautiful widow had already got a job of a waitress in a house near the Court.

Moly had lost her father in an accident while she was ten years old. Both mother and daughter talked English with good British accent.

One morning while Miley was corning out of her room, she saw Moly, in a joyful mood, sweeping the veranda. She was humming a tune-from an old English film.

Miley stood at the door and watched Moly with a frown.

It was her costly and colourful dress that made her frown.

She wore a green silk blouse with golden frills on the sleeves and a green silk skirt with golden lace below.

Miley got irritated at the sight of the maid in such a fantastic fashion while on her cleaning work.

In a loud voice Miley asked.

"Ei, Moly, where did you get this new costly silk dress from? You're not afford to buy one like that."

Moly smiled at Miley in a funny way and answered.

"Why? What's the matter? Can't I wear a dress like this? What in any way that'll affect you, girlie?"

Her question made Miley's heckles rise. She shouted.

"You, creature, did I tell you that you can't wear that stuff? I only asked you where you got it from? Can't you answer that question alone?"

Now Moly was on her knees scrubbing the floor. Miley saw the skirt with golden lace was also being scrubbed.

Moly was ordered by Miley not to make the dress dirty by dragging it along. "Ei, sweeper that's your best bib and tucker."

"Let it get dirty. Who cares? I shall wear it wherever and whenever I wish. Who are you to question me? I don't care your order or advice. I wish to wear it today because Josephine too is wearing it to school today.

That was a surprise news for Miley.

Josephine was a student in her school. She was her friend.

"How d'you come to know of Josephine's dressing code? She is the daughter of Mr. John Brio, the police officer in Anjengo. Who are you to compare Josephine with you, you mean sweeper? D'you go there to sweep her house also, idiot? I hate you! You're despicable. Daft as a brush."

Moly got up from the floor with the wet clothe in her hands and retorted angrily "Don't call me idiot. A cultured girl like you should not use such bad words. It's very rude to stick your tongue out at people like me. I'm poor. But I'm not an idiot. I am not silly. I'm an Englishman's daughter. Anyway to make your concern about my new dress less, I tell you that it was presented to me by Josephine's mummy. Both Josephine and I had the same dress. I'm damn sure that she'll wear her's today. Go and see her in your school." Saying so Moly continued her cleaning job.

Miley described Moly to shama and Cornelia on their way to School.

Her dress, the way she used it on work and about a quarrel they had in the morning, her merry grin, her humming a film tune, all events from beginning to end she narrated. Shama and Cornelia chortled with delight.

"Why are you laughing? It's no laughing matter. It's something very serious. Miley said with a stern face.

"She claimed that Josephine would come to school wearing the dress similar to that of hers. "Miley informed them.

''Let's wait and see Miley. We're on our way to school. Be calm. Let's find out the fact behind the dress after meeting Josephine. Till then keep quiet and get your skates on". Shama orderedher.

Cornelia told them about her doubt.

"Shama, I saw that girl coming out of the inspector's room holding a big mug one day. I doubted nothing at that time. But now I smell a rat."

"She may be a sweeper there also. The mug may be for bringing hot coffee for him. For the time being imagine like that. Please don't spoil this morning by mugging for silly things. We would better hurry or we will be in for it" said Shama in all seriousness.

When they reached school Josephine was waiting on the veranda in front of the guest room for them very anxiously.

Miley's eyes searched her dress for finding the similarity.

But, for her despair, Josephine was clad in blue velvet frock. She cut a dash in her dress.

Josephine ran towards them.

"Good morning everybody, I have been waiting for you for more than half an hour." Josephine greeted her friends merrily.

"Did you come early to day Jos?" asked Shama.

"Yes. I have brought you something very special to taste. Come, let's go to the Home science block, it's a delicious apple pie and some mango pudding. Mamma made them for you only." Josephine told them.

"That's very kind of her." Shama thanked Jospehine's mumma.

"But, I am afraid, I won't taste it. I will feel like vomiting if I eat anything out. The thought of the items makes me heave.

"Never mind, I can consume her share too. I am a gourmet." Trilled Miley. There was enough time for the bell.

They squatted on the floor.

Josphine served them with the items and Shama was given a bar of chocolate to munch while the others were enjoying their pudding and pie.

"Josu, would you know one Moly Fernandus, a sweeper?" Miley enquired about her sweeper.

"No. I don't know" answered Josphine.

"Why? What is the matter? Who is she?" Josephine asked.

"She is Moly, the sweeper in Miley's house. She wore a fashionable, ready-made dress this morning when she came to sweep her house. She said that the dress was presented to her by your mumma. Is it true? She also declared that you too had a dress like that of hers. We want to know the fact." Shama, said.

Miley then gave a short description of Moly's dress, the way she talked, hummed and dragged the skirt in the dirt.

It was an idiotic information to Josephine.

"Yes friends, I too have got a dress like that of hers, Same colour, same texture, the same golden frills and face. It was bought by my father from Madras last week. But there was only one set. How could mother present her one then? My set is with me. Father asked me to wear it today, but I kept it for another occasion in school." Josephine explained.

"How did it come to that spoilt brat then?" asked Miley in astonishment.

"I don't know my dear. We are new to this place. Mumma doesn't know anyone here except the wives of a few officers. She goes clubbing most week ends. There only she has friends. Moreover papa doesn't allow her to mingle with the cheap women in Anjengo." She uttered contemptuously.

"Then how did the dress reach her? We must investigate the case thoroughly." Cornelia stood up and declared.

"But how?" asked the others with thrills and spills.

"We must visit her house this afternoon after our class. We must question her by pointing a sharp knife at her. Let's be the CIB for a day. She may be coerced into answering our questions. What's your opinion, Jose? Do you all agree to do this?" Miley asked them in exhilaration.

"Yes, of course. We all do agree." They stated in unison.

"Let's go to my papa's office first to get his permission,"

Josephine said. "Without his permission I can't go anywhere."

"Okay, Jos, we must have been provided with his reassurance before moving on to an investigation." Stated Shama.

The sound of the last bell of the day thudded into the four hearts. They came out of their classes and assembled in the office veranda. The clock ticked away the minutes. Sisters were moving towards the office for signing their presence in the afternoon.

The four, then, moved out of the school gate and ran towards Mr. John Brio's office to get his permission to visit Moly's house. If he asked 'why' then it would be Miley's turn to explain the reason. Miley had already invented a genuine reason in her mind to satisfy Josephine's father.

But a slight fear and a low level anxiety made them nervous when they neared the office.

The office boy greeted Josphine and told her that her father had already left his office at 3 0'clock.

When the office boy disappeared they four clapped their hands and cried 'Hooray'.

A few policemen heard the children's exclamation and came out to see them. The children ran away by waving their hands to the policemen who were smiling at them and waved back.

Moly's rented house was near the government ware house. Miley directed the others to her house.

They slowly entered her compound. The path to the house was cool and dark with over hanging trees. To their surprise they saw her front yard was full of red roses and white lilies.

"How beautiful! The air is fragrant with scents of rose flower." Exclaimed Shama. "It is a bijou house!"

The front door was bolted from inside.

Instead of ringing the door bell, they thought of going to the kitchen garden to find out any easy access to the inside. They saw an open window with a curtain. Cornelia approached the window.

She slowly moved off the curtain and peeped through the window bars.

It was the bed room window facing the backyard of the house.

Cornelia threw back her head and suddenly moved off from the window.

She went pale and looked at Shama in great surprise after viewing an abysmal scene inside.

Shama, Miley and Josephine ran towards the window to have a view of the bedroom.

There, on the bed, they saw Josephine's father lying over Moly and doing some exercises. Both of them seemed naked.

Cornelia pulled the three off from the window and ordered them to run away from the scene.

"What are they doing there?" Shama asked Cornelia innocently.

Cornelia looked at Josephine. She was pale, sad and looked shocked.

"Keep quiet, Shama I will tell you later."

They ran towards the church.

They were panting heavily. They sat on the lower step of the flight of steps led up to the premises of the church.

They watched one another very strongly. Their faces looked strained and weary. Cornelia spoke in a low strained voice.

"Friends, erase what we saw a minute ago from our minds. We viewed nothing but darkness inside."

Shama wanted to know what the man was doing on her body.

Cornelia felt irritated and said, "They were having sex, you know coitus. What our parents did to produce us. Are you satisfied now with my answer?"

"What cocks do to hens. What dogs do to bitches." said Miley.

Shama sat there without understanding what they were talking about. She was totally bewildered by Cornelia and Miley's comments.

Josephine began to whimper.

"My father! I hate him."

Cornelia took Josepine's head to her breast and patted her on her shoulders pacifyingly.

"My father is a dog. She's a bitch." Josephine cried her heart out. Her friends could not say or do anything to make her calm. They sat down around her helpless and kept their mouths shut for a while.

At last Cornelia warned the others.

"Now let's take a vow not to let others know about the affair. Let's dig holes in our minds and bury the scene into it and cover it with our firmness, so that it may get decomposed there and should not be allowed to permeate the gas through the air. That means we must forget everything about that. We haven't seen anything. We don't know anything. Now take a vow not to let anybody know of this. Josephine, my dear forget everything. Don't tell this to your mamma, please. That'll break your family as well as your mumma's heart."

Cornelia made Josephine to stand up and they all promised that they would keep everything secret.

Shama and Miley ran towards the ferry as the time was nearing to 5'0 Clock.

They did not want their parents to be in a state of panic about their delay.

Cornelia accompanied Josephine to her house. Cornelia waited at the gate and said good bye to Josephine when she entered her house.

When Cornelia reached home, it was half past five. She tried her level best to confirm Alex that her delay was due to her volley ball practice in school.

For the first time in her life she told a white lie. Her conscience pricked her as she lied to her brother.

\* \* \* \* \* \* \*

## CHAPTER 11

# ON THE HORNS OF A DILEMMA

L isa, Josephine's mumma paced up and down outside the house hotly since half past four. She was tensed up about her daughter's delay.

When Josephine appeared at the gate at five minutes past five she heaved a sigh of relief.

She caught a glimpse of cornelia taking leave of her daughter. She stared at Josephine and grilled her about why she came late and where she had been till five five. "I have been on pins and needles all the time waiting for your arrival." Josephine observed her mother's perplexed expression.

She felt her heartbeat quicken as she approached her saintly mother.

She was saddened to see her being cheated by her philandering husband. A dog upon a bitch!.

She thought for a while. What would be the after effects if she came to know that her husband was having an affair with a sweeper! "Oh, it's terrible and unthinkable" Josephine tried her best to bring a faint smile on her parched lips.

Lisa shouted at her.

"Where were you after your school hours? Loitered on the coast of Anjengo with those nasty girls?"

Josephine became very heated and shouted back,

Please mind your words, mumma. They are not nasty girls. They are from very high families, higher than that of yours.

But Lisa went on.

"Don't you remember your papa's strict instructions about your timing in your day to day work? Don't you know that he is so temperamental? We never know what to expect with him.

He will do his nut when he finds out your late arrival. Thank God! "Anyhow you came back before he reached home."

Josephine retorted in a disgruntled manner.

"Don't expect your husband till eight in the evening. He is very busy with his fishy dealings near the warehouse. He's in a roll in the hay".

The scene of the affair made Josephine quiver with anger. Thank God! Her mother did not hear the last sentence.

"Fishy dealings? What fishy dealings? What d'you mean by that? How'd you come to know of any of his dealings, eh?" Lisa questioned her very angrily.

Josephine felt a cold shiver of fear run through her. She tried her best to remain calm. She commented to her mother.

"Nothing Mamma. I simply want to see your crimson face. You look more beautiful when you get angry. I'm leaving you mumma for my chamber. I'd like a wash and need a freshening up." Saying that much, she ran to her room. At present her room was a bolt-hole for her.

Josephine lay down on the bed without changing her school dress.

Her school books had been spread out on the bed.

She lay down on her front and thrust her face into the soft pillow and started whimpering.

After half an hour Lisa entered the room with a cup of hot tea.

The tea-cup trembled in her hand when she spotted her dear daughter in such a grievous condition.

Lisa felt she was loosing her grip.

Josephine was beating her face against the pillow.

Lisa kept the tea cup on a stool in a corner and ran towards her daughter. She lifted her daughter's head and gathered Josephine to her.

"My poor mumma! My poor mumma! She moaned and groaned while hugging Lisa.

"Oh, my poor child! What had happened to you dear? I scolded you because I'm afraid of your father. Why did you come late, daughter? I saw that Cornelia with you at the gate. Was there anything happened on your way home? "I'm, very much worried. Tell me Jos what's the problem that grips you, child? Share it with me. I'm your loving mumma."

Josephine embraced her mother more tightly and kissed her warmly.

Lisa's woe-be-gone face made Josephine start whimpering again.

Lisa panicked and felt a little groggy.

Josephine noticed her mother's condition and in order to make her regain her calmness she said, "nothing to worry mumma I've had a long hard day practicing volleyball at school. We're going to compete with the St. Joseph's team next month."

Josephine stammered while lying to her mother and darted a painful look at her. She continued.

"Sorry, mumma. I've made you come with the tea. My head's blazing with a hard ache. Would you mind allowing me to sleep a little, mumma? Only less than half an hour I'll take to lie down."

Lisa admitted her request with a shake of her head.

"All right my dear, take rest after drinking this tea Oh, it's too cold for your liking. I'll heat it again and give you."

Lisa went to the kitchen and made another cup of tea and came back to see that her daughter had already gone to a deep sleep. She left her daughter without disturbing.

But Lisa was very anxious to know the reason for her daughter's sudden head ache and her grief. She asked herself the question

"Why was she late? Why Cornelia accompanied her home?"

A sudden thought flashed through her mind.

Josephine turned thirteen in June. She has exceptionally grown. Has she turned matured? Is the first menstrual blood that disturbs her?

Lisa ran back to Josephine's room. She had fallen into a deep slumber.

Lisa turned Josephine to a side and checked her panties and petticoat. There were no symptoms of that.

Lisa came to know that it was not the reason for her disturbance and shaken up.

The mother went to the prayer room and knelt down to pray for her only daughter.

"May God be with my child. Please God, don't make her sad and unhappy. My innocent little brille is my everything in this world. I pray for your blessings."

Every now and again Lisa went into her room and checked to see if she was still asleep. At about a quarter past six Josephine got up from her sleep and went to the bathroom to have a bath in cold water. She changed her dress and made herself up.

She calmed her mind herself and went to her study.

She completed her homework and got immersed herself in her daily lessons.

An hour passed.

She heard her father's voice down stairs.

John Brio's Loud guffaw evoked Josephine's memory of his immoral act and she threw away her books, papers, pens and pencils from the table and ran to the bathroom and shut herself in.

"Oh, Jesus, please erase those scenes from my mind and indelibly imprint your crucifix there. I can't face my vicious father," Josephine began to hit her head against the door.

John Brio was in a jovial mood.

He came into her room to wish her as usual. "Hello, my pretty little Josu! Where are you my child?"

He heard thuds from inside the bathroom.

He dashed towards the bathroom door and knocked hard at it.

"Josu, open the door. What's the thud? What are you doing there? What a mess in your study?"

Josephine felt embarrassed and uncomfortable about the hard knocking.

She opened the door. She could not stand the sight of him. She cringed in terror and flipped her lid.

"I hate you, You're despicable. Get out of my room and get lost you Moly's dog. You may sometimes forget that I'm your daughter, you son of a bitch. You may try to do the thing to me too as you have done to that bitch this afternoon!? A dog upon a bitch! I hate you. Go and live with that Moly. You presented her a dress just like that of mine! Who's she to you, your wife? your keep? your daughter? Your're an immoral and impious creature going on cheating my poor mumma. Get out and get lost you philanderer. You're a mad dog and if you stand in front of me I'll shoot you with your service revolver. Get lost you fornicator."

She screamed her lungs out and fell down on the floor unconscious.

John Brio got frightened and called his wife aloud.

"Lisa, Lisa, come here soon."

He gathered his daughter's body and put her on the bed. He took water from the jug and sprinkled on her face.

Lisa was lighting candles in the prayer room. Hearing her husband's alarming call, She made a dash for Josephine's room. Josephine opened her eyes and saw her father holding her to his breast and crying.

She felt pity for him.

She glanced up quickly to see her mother frantic with worry.

She wanted to go with the flow and wished a lot to avoid a family quarrel.

"Oh, papa! How are you?" Josephine hugged her father and enquired friendly to please her mumma.

John Brio was too stunned to speak.

Lisa watched papa and daughter in wonder and amusement.

"What's going on between papa and daughter?"

John Brio kissed his daughter and laid her down on the bed.

He just couldn't stop crying.

He gathered his wife and took her head to his breast and said, "our one and only child".

I don't need any worldly pleasures except you two. My daughter is my everything. Your're my treasures. Lisa, don't hate me.

Dear Jose, I beg your pardon girlie.

Oh Jesus, trample me to death for my sin. I want my daughter. I want my family" He went on murmuring. Lisa was touched by his solicitude for them.

He groaned with shame solidly for half an hour. Josephine rose up from bed and gave John "Brio a cuddle. She whispered, "Sorry papa," in his ear.

Lisa was actually perplexed by the sight of both father and daughter apologizing each other.

"What's the problem? Why did she fall down unconscious a minute ago? What shocks you, such an imposing man? Why are you crying your eyes out? What are you lamenting about?" Lisa put forward a volley of angry questions to him.

Josephine cuddled her and said,

"Nothing mumma. You know I was severely suffering from a bad head ache. When I heard father's voice downstairs I suddenly got up from bed. That speedy rising up made my head swirl and I fell fainted."

But John Brio did not want to give any explanation. He left home without even changing his uniform.

He walked towards his office and stayed there all night.

He was boozing out his fear about his daughter's knowledge that he had a coitus with Moly. He hated himself and asked himself a lot of questions on how she came to know of that affair. If Lisa was informed of that, what his family life would be afterwards and so on and so forth. So he drugged up to his eyeballs.

He cursed his life of depravity.

He thought that he had been bonking many young women and even his subordinate officers' wives who were yielding to him.

John Brio felt depressed about the future of his beloved daughter.

He knelt down and started to sob uncontrollably.

"Oh, God send me into a sudden death. I deserve to have innumerable whiplashes till I fall down dead. I've no more courage to face my wife and daughter. I've been philandering ever since I reached my manhood and now I am caught redhanded by my daughter! Oh, I don't want to live anymore."

John Brio suddenly took out his revolver to shoot himself. While he was keeping his finger on the trigger he heard a peal of church bells ringing out and his revolver fell down from his hand.

The heavy sound of the morning bell sent a shiver down his spine.

He rose up from his kneeling position and slowly walked out of the room and started for the church as if he were in a dream.

He genuflected and attended the service.

He went to a confession. Father Bernard, the senior priest heard his confession. Later the priest invited him to his chamber and had a friendly talk.

Father Bernard advised him to go on a pilgrimage to holy places with his family to get rid of the present mental distress and to retrieve his former state of mind. It was father Bernard who saved John Brio's blushes.

It was a quarter past seven in the morning when John Brio reached home. He looked pale and haggard.

Lisa was giving instructions to her servant in the kitchen. She was kneading flour for making chapatti for breakfast.

He went upstairs and watched his daughter still sleeping. He did not want to wake her up. He stood rooted there for some time thinking about what he should do next.

His eyes were red and swollen from crying and skipping supper and sleep.

He went downstairs and called Lisa to come to him.

Lisa washed her hands and went running towards her husband.

He asked her to sit on the sofa beside him.

He was searching in his mind for apt words for a perfect start to the conversation. "I want to let you know something very serious. You know that your husband's not a perfect man.

I was a wayward.

I'm a wayward. But I promise you that I will be a perfect gentleman, a good husband, and a good father in future. He was on the verge of tears.

You have been bearing my callousness, my brutality my immorality and my drunkenness ever since our nuptial mass ceremony and ever since you entered into my room as a bride.

If any other woman were there in your place she would have divorced me and left me forever.

But you're different and you love me a lot. Look Lisa, now I repent of what I have done so far and I promise, you that I will lead a good life and become a trust worthy husband, a creditable and dedicated father to our dear daughter.

I confess you that yesterday somehow or other Josephine came to know of my affair. That was the reason for all the troubles.

Our Josephine is going to be a mature girl in the near future and I should lead a pure life.

Could you, Lisa, please pardon me? If you couldn't I'll surely put an end to my life now." Lisa got frightened and embraced her husband warmly and sobbed.

"Please don't utter such rude words. I won't be able to face such things. My mother is my role model. She had advised me a lot about how to behave in a husband's house, how to deal with things and cope up with the stresses and strains in a married life. Some men are like you. Even my father used to take drinks and he had many illegal affairs.

She often suspected her husband, my father, that he had committed adultery. Even then her family life went on smoothly and her compatibility with her husband paved the way to her success in life as an able wife and a successful mother of seven children. I saw my mother with a smiling face only even though she had to face many personal adversities in her life.

I decided to follow my mother's practical outlook on life. I've been praying to the Almighty to change you and, now I'm the happiest of all wives in the world.

It's the result of my tears that I shed in front of the crucifix. Thank God." John Brio felt relieved.

"D' you think you could change your uniform and have a wash in warm water? I'll bathe you, if you want- 'Please don't be a doleful looking person here afterwards'

John Brio obeyed her like a baby.

Josephine had a slight fever and so she was not allowed to go to school that day. Joshn Brio said to Lisa,

"Lisa, I could eat a horse."

She ran to the kitchen and asked the servant to set the table for breakfast.

"A hearty breakfast is served. Come soon." Lisa called out.

Lisa's voice awoke Josephine, she got up from her bed and moved slowly towards the bathroom to brush her teeth. She needed to change and clean up.

Her parents were having breakfast when she came down to join them.

They exchanged greetings.

Josephine didn't eat much breakfast. But when John Brio informed them that they were going on a pilgrimage that evening, she began to devour.

Lisa and Josephine were very happy to hear the mind blowing information.

Josephine thanked God for giving her an opportunity to evade her friends who had caught sight of her father's adultery. She wished herself a million miles away.

The pilgrimage at this time would be a panacea, she thought. They got ready for the journey and in the evening at about seven they started on a pilgrimage.

Week by week John Brio grew mentally stronger and he decided to send his leave application to the British head quarters in Madras.

He had applied for three months leave and requested the authorities for a transfer to the Ooty police station.

After three months he was transferred to Ooty and Josephine was admitted in a reputed school there.

She had to attend a severe test in the school. She passed the test with high marks. The school authorities were pleased with her test results and she was allowed to join eighth form in the next academic year.

\* \* \* \* \* \* \*

## Chapter 12
# Miley's Pleasant Surprise

The annual examination was over, Shama, Miley and Cornelia were promoted to Seven A.

They felt sorry for Josephine who could not attend the exam as she had been on leave.

One day, the officer in charge informed Shama that their friend Josephine had got admission in eighth form in a famous school in Ooty. He told her that the Inspector, Mr. John Brio had been transferred to Ooty station as Superintendent of Police. The officer also informed her that he had changed a lot in his behavior towards freedom fighters.

Miley seemed in jovial spirits as her only one brother Lorrence arrived from Ooty to spend his summer vacation with his parents and sister. Her grandma and granddad had come with him.

Lorrence was studying in a famous British school in Ooty. He was doing his matriculation there.

He was a boarder there and came home for the holidays along with his grand parents in Ooty.

Lorrence was the embodiment of the successful young studious man. He was a voracious reader. He was desirous of taking part in sports and games. He hit big in winning gold medals for swimming international at the age of fifteen. He was then seventeen. His graceful body was the result of his

Calisthenics. One day Miley told him all about Josephine and her father John Brio. She showed him her recent photograph and said.

"See, brother, this is Josephine. Shama told me that she had been admitted in a famous school in Ooty. Could you please search her out. I missed her greatly.

"She looks sweet and comely in this photograph. I think she's photogenic. She's a dead ringer for a girl I used to know in our music class. He complimented Josephine on her physical attractiveness.

"She looks sweeter and more attractive, brother. You'll find out the fact when you see her in the flesh." Miley began to describe her features and her most cherishable and cherubic character and nature.

"All right, sister. I'll try my level best to locate her and convey your message. But I must know which school she has been admitted in. There are four or five famous English schools in Ooty. My school is the most internationally famous one. I think she might have sought admission there. Anyway let me seek her out."

Lorrence returned to Ooty after the summer holidays. He thought of going through the list of newly admitted pupils in his school first, before going searching the where abouts of Miley's friend in other schools.

The clerk, Mr. Samuel helped Lorrence to trace Josephine's name in the list. She was admitted in eighth form A division. Lorrence felt relieved and thanked God. Lorrence showed Josephine's photograph to the headmaster of the school and entreated him to allow him to meet the girl in his presence to convey his sister's regards to her.

Josephine was called to the headmaster's room during the morning recess. Lorrence was waiting to see her with mixed emotions.

Josephine entered the headmaster's room nervously. He welcomed her and introduced Lorrence to her.

"This is your Anjengo friend Miley's brother Lorrence. He wanted to convey his sister's love and regards to you. Lorrence is the best student of this school. You move to that side room and converse."

Lorrence and Josephine went to the side room. It embarrassed Josephine to meet a young boy in the room. But she regained her dignity and greeted him warmly.

"Hello, Miley's brother, how're you?'

Lorrence was elated at the sight of a beauty queen in front of him. Her sweet, slim, stylish and gracious appearance helped developed an affection for her in his heart.

He was charmed by her beauty and vivacity.

Josephine waited for his response.

She looked at him eagerly.

"I' m fine, thank you." He responded by feeling shy over his delay in responding her greeting.

Josephine admired his inconceivably attractive, strong and handsome features.

Lorrence was attracted to her by her magnetic smile.

They stood looking at each other for a while and Josephine started the conversation.

"How's Miley?"

"She's fine. She had missed you a lot. The trident is grieving on your absence."

"I too feel sad. What to do? Did Miley tell you anything about my father?"

Josephine asked him mildly.

"Oh, forget about that. Now come to the point.

D' you like this school? How d' you get along with your studies? Have you got any friends here?"

Josephine laughed heartily and said to him.

"I'm trying to get on very well. I've just got a friend; that's you, Miley's brother. As far as my studies are concerned I feel a little difficult to follow the lessons here.

Now the ice of silence and strangeness melted down and they became more warm and friendly.

Lorrence talked a lot about the school subjects, the school projects, sports activities and co-curricular activities.

"I'm the captain of the swimming club here. I just live and breathe swimming" said Lorrence lively.

Josephine smiled at him and took a shine to him.

She stated proudly.

"I'm an ardent volleyball player. I like to join the team here." I've taken to volleyball playing like a duck to water.

You can join the team here. I'll see to it. Right Josephine, the bell has gone. Let's part for the day. We can meet again next Friday afternoon. I'll try to get the headmaster's permission for our next meeting."

"Thank you very much. May I leave?"

''Yes, of course."

Josephine went to her class.

She could not concentrate on her studies.

"A boy of considerable stature!'

The most handsome one I've ever seen."

Josephine became completely obsessive about Lorrence.

Lorrenee wrote a long letter to Miley describing how he felt at that moment when he met Josephine in his school. "I have great admiration for her and I think I fell in love with her. The moment of our meeting was just a foretaste of what is to come. Josephine's beauty and her smile are stamped indelibly on my mind.

I'm waiting to come of my age to request my parents to propose her for me. I hope she would be my life mate.

Lorrence's words in the letter were very creditable and Miley submitted the letter to her parents for their perusal.

They laughed their head off after going through it.

Miley's father replied remarkably that he would see to the matter positively if he pass the civil service examination with flying colours.

"Concentrate fully on your studies now and persevere in getting good marks in your matriculation examination and try to get training in the civil services then. No love affair until then. But I assure you that I would ask John Brio for his daughter's hand in marriage for you the moment you emerge as a key figure in the ICS officers' selection. So now set your mind and heart only to attain that aim. When time comes I'll allow you to go down the aisle".

Lorrence laughed at his idiotic feeling and began to work hard to attain his goal in life.

Josephine and Lorrence met up on all Friday afternoons and exchanged their ideas and information. By degrees their friendship grew into love.

He often watched her practising volleyball on the playground. They exchanged glances and sometimes she ran to him and kiss him on both cheeks.

At times Lorrence blushed with shame. Sometimes he was positively beaming with pleasure.

They shared their feelings, their decision and their teenage romance. Lorrence and Josephine seemed made for each other.

One day Josephine got a chance to meet him alone in the library.

Lorrence, being a voracious reader was sitting there with an important reference book. He immersed himself in his work.

Josephine tiptoed over to the seat in front of him and sat there silently for more than ten minutes watching him reading and writing the notes out on a paper.

She tilted her head back and looked up at him with a smile. While moving she played footsie With him and drew his attention.

Lorrence held his head up and saw her sitting in front of him smiling.

"Hello, dear. How're you?"

"I'm fine. Thank you."

"Haven't you got class?"

"This is a free period. I came here to 'browse the shelves for something interesting to read.

I saw you reading and writing down notes. I think you're preparing well for your matriculation examination.

"yes, darling. I have a hectic schedule. By the way d' you read morning papers everyday?"

"No, I get no time to go through the dailies." Lorrence advised her to read daily newspapers and get herself familiarized with the new political trends.

Lorrence gave her a lecture on the Indians' fight against British for the freedom of India. She listened to him, entranced.

"Our national leaders as well as the common citizens are fighting and whole heartedly receiving arrests and willingly staying in prisons. Some are being killed by the British rulers.

Have you heard about the wagon tragedy and other atrocities done to Indians to put a stop to their fight? Indians are fighting without violence.

The national leaders are going to form an assembly to frame the Indian constitution.

Haven't you heard of Bim Rao Ramji Ambedkar? It is he who is framing our constitution.

The members of the assembly met on December nine and decided to do many important things in free India."

"Is our country going to get freedom shortly?" Josephine asked very eagerly.

"Yes of course. The British will leave our country soon. My birthday is on August twenty six. I wish I would celebrate my eighteenth birthday in free India.

Josephine was elated to hear a detailed description of the present condition of the country.

But she was very sorry for her father's different view about the freedom movement and he hated Jawaharlal Nehru, Mahatma Gandhi and other national leaders.

John Brio supported the British and told her that it was because of the English men in India the Indians became literate and cultured in their outlook.

"My father says that he won't live in India if the Britishers leave the place. He's thinking of moving to England after the Independence. He says he will try to get English citizenship in England. He'll take my mother and I there as an emigrant family." She said in a pathetic tone.

Lorrence assured her that he would meet her father and make him understand the changes that are taking place in their mother land and force him to bestow his service to his motherland.

"I'm damn sure that he would agree with me and consider my opinion. You can very well wait for his considered opinion." Lorrence declared.

"My father's no more stubborn in his outlook of life after that Moly's episode. He changed a lot. He may accept your view of life and modern findings.'" Josephine stated sadly.

"You know, Josephine, My sister had written to me everything about your father. But then I didn't know anything about your character and conduct. Now I love and respect you for your real personality. After completing my education and fulfilling my parents' wish and ambition about my career as an ICS officer I'll, Surely ask your father for your hand in marriage.

But I want you too to strive for reaching the highest position which you like the best. Only through hard work and great diligence in our school work that we can achieve success in life." Josephine was captivated. She rose up from her seat and approached him. She embraced him warmly and promised in his ear that she would try to get high marks in all classes.

She told him that she wants to be an eminent doctor.

She kissed him with an unusual fervour and ran off the library hall before anyone comes in.

Josephine felt excited.

She felt as if she were in a paradise of love floating in the hands of Lorrence with her arms round his body, kissing each other and flowing slowly towards their life's destination.

Alerted by the teacher's sudden question, Josephine stood up, looked puzzled and began to grope for the right answer.

The teacher got irritated and scolded her a lot for being inattentive in the class.

Josephine was deeply ashamed of her behavior in the class and her face was ashen and wet with sweat. She made a firm decision not to repeat her absent mindedness in class again.

Next time when they met Lorrence repeated his advice and got an assurance from her that she would work hard to attain A+ grades in her exams.

"You're a very brilliant girl, and you can pass the exams with flying colours as well as you can shine in your sports and in extra curricular activities. Success is within your grasp.

You can earn a name and I wish to see you in a great position in future.

Josephine gave him her word that she would never be the despair of him.

"Now may I ask you for something very valuable for me?" Josephine entreated him.

"What's that my sweetie'?" Lorrence asked her with a smile.

"Something which I have been craving to get from you". Saying that she pointed towards her rosy cheek and closed her eyes for a moment.

Lorrence looked around to make Sure that no one was in the vicinity and gave her a warm kiss on her forehead. But she pointed again to her cheeks. Lorrence cupped her face in his hands and kissed her.

Lorrence now felt the warmth of her arms around him. But he slowly let go of her hands and informed her. "Our meeting and every thing we do is pre ordained.

"But be careful dear. Students and staff are around us. What do they think of us? Thank God. Nobody noticed anything. Come on let us move towards our blocks.

The dewy-eyed Josephine said softly.

"My heart's beating for you only.

Goodbye and have a good day."

She ran towards the western block where the seventh and eighth forms work.

Josephine from that day onwards seemed totally absorbed in her school work. Josephine wrote a long letter to Miley describing everything about her school, the curriculum, new life and a little about her love affair.

"I'm fourteen, I've visibly blossomed over the last few months. My friendship with your brother blossomed into love. This is between you, me and the gatepost.

I take you as my future sister-in-law and I'm opening my 'mind to you. I don't know whether you accept me or not. I expect that you won't desert me. Miley, I dream a lot. My heart is in your brother's hands.

I think he won't break it.

Miley, please don't let your parents come to know of my confession. I don't want them to curse me for trapping their only one son who always aspires everything great.

I wish I'd reached the marriageable age so soon that I could be his better half.

Please don't laugh at me. Miley. You'll experience the same feelings when you reach my age and when you meet a heartthrob one day.

Under no circumstances should you let Shama and Cornelia know about my affair. They would think that I'm just like my father.

My love towards your brother is genuine and I breathe in not oxygen but I breathe in his faith for the existence of my life.

Your brother is loved and respected by everyone here. The school authorities have very high opinion about him. He's the best student and the best athlete here. He's bold, morally stable and duty minded. He maintains order and very creditable.

All students and teachers have love and respect for him. Girls in his class are always after him. I hate them. But Lorrence is a perfect gentleman.

How fortunate you are, Miley, to have a brother like him. He's a treasure. I've no words to describe his knowledge and wisdom.

I pray to Jesus for your health and well being and I pray for your parents' health and long life. They are my Lorrence's parents. So they are mine too.

Now the Moly's episode glances on my mind. I thank Moly now 'It was a blessing in disguise. It is my debauched papa's rakish behavior that led me to my present situation and chanced a meeting with your brother and the soaring of my spirits due to our everlasting love.

I conclude my letter by reminding you once again not to let anyone know of my love affair with your brother. Please don't let the cat out of your bag.

My love is divine and I decided to work hard to reach a high position professionally and personally to please my lover. If I am deserted in future, I'll surely put a full stop to my life without any sort of rethinking.

Please keep everything in your mind and don't tell anything about this to your parents or relatives. Your loving Josephine."

Miley completed reading that sensational words in writing with tears of joy and shock in her eyes.

She hugged the precious letter to her chest for sometime. She tried not to let slip what she knew.

It was a pleasant surprise to Miley. She began to imagine the scenes of a future wedding and Josephine's arrival to their home as her beloved sister-in-law. She kept the letter as an important love manifesto secretly among her other valuable treasures, She never told anything to anybody. It was only her own pleasant surprise. Miley's letter was not scrutinized in the school by the headmistress as the sender was Josephine.

The headmistress too got a letter from Josephine explaining the method of teaching, the accent, the curriculum, the strict discipline and the quiet and calm atmosphere, the clean premises, the hectic schedule, the etiquette followed by the inmates, students and staff and so an and so forth in her school.

All the nuns have been given a chance to go through her scholarly, scintillating and neat script and they talked about it in admiration. They thought that her departure from their institution was a great loss to the school.

The nuns of the sacred heart loved the girl and they prayed for her well being. The Anjengo people were completely unaware of the Moly-John Brio incident.

Most of them thought that he was transferred suddenly because the British government had got fed up with his inhuman and brutal treatment of the commons, the criminals and his subordinates in his circle.

But only Moly Fernandus knew the reason and she stopped working in Miley's house. John Brio had got that innocent girl into trouble.

Father Bernard called her out and warned her against unworthiness and advised her to lead a life of virtue. After that she had to go into hiding for several months and none but father Bernard knew that Moly Fernandus had given birth to a healthy baby boy in a distant convent with a dominant gene of John Brio. The boy was a chip off the old block.

\* \* \* \* \* \* \*

# Chapter 13
# The Sensational Seeing - Off

The 'Quit India' was a country wide movement. The masses got involved in the movement.

The bravery and heroic deeds of many people in India were to be admired.

Many had perished nameless in the fight for freedom.

Everybody contributed his or her share for the freedom of their motherland. A meeting of minds could be witnessed everywhere.

The situation in India was very serious at that time.

Lord Mount Batten came to India as the viceroy.

He presented a plan to alleviate the problem.

The plan was to divide the country into two separate nations- India and Pakistan. Hindu-Muslim riots had started in different parts of the country.

Communal riots led to the killings of many innocent people and Mahatma Gandhi went on a fast unto death to end the mind less and frenzied killings.

The British passed the India Independence Act of July 1947.

India got her freedom on August 15, 1947 and the country was partitioned.

At the stroke of midnight hour, when the whole world slept, India was awake to life and freedom.

On August 26 Lorrence came home to celebrate his eighteenth birth day.

He blew the candles on a cream cake out in the presence of his parents, nan and granddad, other relatives and friends. Shama and Cornelia too were specially invited to attend his birthday celebration.

All had a blowout and the guests presented Lorrence with special gifts.

Shama gifted him with a very beautiful bouquet and Cornelia presented him with a general knowledge book.

Lorrence thanked the guests and retired to his room to write a letter to his fiancée.

Josephine, at that time, was in the chapel kneeling in front of the crucifix and praying for her fiancé.

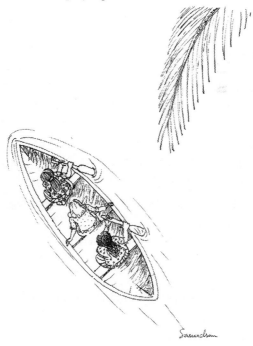

The English in Anjengo were busy leaving the place for their native place after the independence.

The village then came under the rule of the congress government.

The Maharaja of Travancore became powerless and was presented with a privy purse for his use.

The little children of Anjengo celebrated their Independence Day in a very fitting manner. They went on a procession holding the national flags and singing the national anthem.

The British nuns left the sacred heart and the school then was handed over to the Indian nuns to run. The school decided to follow the Indian curriculum.

Lady Mary was preparing to leave the country.

She had sold her property lock stock and barrel to a rich merchant of Travancore. He allowed the English lady to use the mansion and feel free there until she left for England.

Lady Mary loved India and the Indians especially the fisher folk of Anjengo.

She used to help the poor and needy there.

Shama, Miley and Cornelia visited her on a Sunday afternoon.

They came to her with a big chocolate cake and a bunch of sweet smelling flowers.

Lady Mary informed the girls that she was leaving Anjengo after a week.

Cornelia was presented with her sewing machine. She had long coveted to get one like that.

She gazed at her most cherished possession in amazement.

Cornelia felt exhilarated and knelt down and kissed Lady Mary's hands with respect and affection.

She thanked her for the costly present.

Lady Mary gifted Miley with a new set of costly earrings.

Shama was presented with some story books. The children thanked her and said. We're very sorry to miss you.

You were a solace to us.

Where do we go for good advice in your absence, mam?

May God bless you.

We pray for your safe journey and a happy life in England." Shama said with sadness.

Lady Mary was deeply moved by her words.

"We start our journey to London from here next Monday morning at about ten. We go to Bombay by train. From there we board our ship to our destination.

We like Indians and their culture. You, the little children of Anjengo are intelligent and lively. Your words and actions will live with me all my life. I wish you to be here on Monday morning to see us off."

Lady Mary took them to their inner room and forced them enjoy, her Yorkshire pudding. Shama was given an apple to munch on.

With nods and smile they took leave of Lady Mary and other members of her family.

Shama told Gaya and Gauri about Lady Mary's departure on Monday morning.

Six days are left for her to continue in India.

Gaya and Gauri reminded Shama about Cornelia's future and told her to meet Lady Mary and request her to take Cornelia too to England as her adopted daughter.

So Shama visited Lady Mary the next day.

The white lady welcomed her.

"Madam, I come to you again to discuss something very important. It's about Cornelia. She's a talented girl and if she gets good Education in a foreign country she'll emerge as a well known figure in future.

Could you please adopt Cornelia as your child and educate her there in England, Mam? She'll pass the exams with flying colours.

If she continues her study there, she'll get a good profession there and thereby she can support her big family. Jesus may bless you, mam, if you do this favour to this poor but scholarly girl.

She's very kind hearted and she may be a great help to you there. She doesn't hesitate to take up any chores in your house.

She can look after your ageing mother too.

Her four siblings are very good children and their progress in life depends on her prosperity and success in life. What do you think about this, Mam? Forgive me if I disturb you and waste your valuable time with this matter. I'm only an eleven year old girl and I don't know whether I'm talking a sensible thing to an important personality like you." Shama looked into Lady Mary's eyes with a melting expression.

Lady Mary appreciated Shama's laudable attempt to find a way of reaching out to Cornelia.

"It's a wonderful idea!" Lady Mary enthused.

"But Shama, did you get their consent? Did her father tell you anything about this? I can take her to England without any adoption. I'm unmarried and sometimes I may get married after reaching my homeland.

But I promise you that I'll take her to England as a sponsor for her education there. First you go and get a written permission from Cornelia, her brothers and sisters and her father. Ask them to meet me tomorrow itself if they are willing. Then only I can proceed to get her a passport and other related papers for her emigration.

My mother will be very happy to get Cornelia to give her company. She'll permit me to take her there.

Shama thanked Lady Mary and rushed out to meet Lazar and Cornelia.

Her efforts gained success. Lazar agreed and gave a written permission allowing Cornelia to be emigrated.

Lady Mary was seen off on the bank of the backwater by the whole lot and waved good bye to her while the family was getting on to a private boat and they waved back.

The sacred heart's atmosphere had entirely been changed after the Independence.

The prayer and the greeting song were changed and the authorities introduced the National Anthem and Vande Matharam in the place of the poem in praise of the British Queen.

The question papers set for the second term examination were not according to the British curriculum. The change in syllabus and schedule could not be accepted by the students.

The parents and children requested the congress government to allow them to complete the academic year by following the old syllabus and curriculum. After writing their final examination in the old pattern they could very well accept the change.

But the government turned a deaf ear to their suggestion and the change in the middle of the year put the children between the devil and the deep sea. Some children took TC and joined in Malayalam Medium schools in Travancore.

The Home Science, the Public Health and Civics were removed from the curriculum and there introduced a new subject called basic education.

The students had to spin thread using unsophisticated spinning wheels operated with hand.

Shama and Miley found it very difficult to follow the new curriculum. Teaching in some subjects had been well below par.

On January 1947 Shama's father, Vishnu, came home to take his family to America. His arrival caused a flurry excitement, He had got a month's leave. He wanted to make the necessary arrangement for their departure.

Shama could not bear the thought of leaving her friends and her grandfather. She was not able to find a way of circumventing her father's plan.

She was in a fit

Her heart was stricken with grief.

But her mother Kamini was in great happiness. She entertained her husband with unusual fervour.

The whole house was in a festive mood. Kamini did the travel arrangements with a gusto. She cooked special items for her husband and she made different sweets for afters. Fruit salad was her special item which Vishnu liked the best.

There was an amused look on the face of grandfather. When he noticed Kamini's change from a desolate and doleful looking lady, often aggressive and moody, to an alive and kicking lassie with an alluring smile and from a pale face with bloodless lips to a rosy and blissful appearance.

Grandfather breathed a sigh of relief.

It was he who forced his son to take his family too to America and lead a feel-good life, there.

He wrote to his son about his wife's condition. The thought that her husband was away leading a lonely life in a strange country among strange people made her feel utterly desolate.

He saw her sitting with a lugubrious face and brooding over what her husband would eat there, how he had been toiling for them, and who would be there to take care of him!! Then grandpa wanted his son and wife to be reunited so badly.

Grandfather signalled visakha to come to him. When Visakha came to him he pointed his finger in Kamini's direction and said.

"Look, your sister came alive when she saw her husband after a period of two long years! Poor girl! Let her enjoy life with her man and child."

Visakha thanked him.

"That's very kind of you, father. You're a great man indeed! So loving and kind hearted. I know that Kamini was not at all happy in her husband's absence. But she did not want to leave you alone in this big house. That was the main reason for vishnu's decision to keep his family here even after getting a green cared."

There arrived many of their relatives and friends to call on Vishnu. The house was fully laden and so Shama, Gaya and Gauri had to occupy the attic.

Shama was very unhappy. She sat alone for hours on the bank of the backwater just gazing into space.

Sometimes she spent her time inside the pergola for Jasmine sulking and sobbing. She did not want to meet anyone.

She hated the guests.

After an hour on sober reflection, she came out of the pergola with a handful of Jasmine. She saw her cousins running towards her.

"Shama, your father wants you. The guests are asking for you. They want to meet you. Go to your father soon."

Shama stared stonily at them for a minute.

When they left her she gave out a sigh of relief, walked home to meet her father. But she stopped short when she heard her name called and saw to her surprise that Gaya and Gauri came running towards her hooting with laughter. They seemed very excited and wanted to reveal a very important information to Shama.

"Our father's been released after the independence and he's reinstated with a higher grade in his post. He informs that he'll be promoted as the Director of Medical instruction very soon.

The government wants our father to be a member of the Ministry of Health in Bombay. But father refused the position with thanks because he likes to serve the poor and needy by imparting medical aid to every nook and cranny of the state.

Mumma got a telegram from him a week ago. She kept it as a secret and waited for your father to arrive because she wanted to explode all into a pleasant surprise.

Now our house is full of mirth and enjoyment. All are in an expansive mood.

You know Shama, we're leaving next week. Father has got a limousine and the vehicle will be here to take us back to Bomaby." Gaya said to Shama.

Gouri said,

"Sister, how alien were we here you know? We've been feeling like a fish out of water for the last several months.

We're very much thankful to you for your sincere love and care and also express our love for grandpa and Kamini aunt to take care of us."

Shama replied.

"Why d'you thank for all these? It's everyone's duty to look after you. We're blood relatives. This is our ancestral home. Your father and' my father are brothers. Your mother and my mother are twins. So we are one.

Now I come to know that you were not happy here. You've been grieving under this roof. Why didn't you share your sorrows, griefs and discontentment with me too. I'm your sister not an outsider. Why did you feel cold aloof and distant in your approach to me. We were not like this before." Saying that much Shama started to weep.

Gaya and Gauri together cuddled and kissed Shama to make her stop weeping and the three then ran home to meet the guests.

After lunch Shama went to her usual resting place near the bank of the backwater. She sat on the lower most branch of the guava tree and began to swing.

She began to recall the gloomy and discontent nature of Gaya and Gauri.

"Why didn't I notice their stress? Why didn't I give them mental support? Why didn't I induce them to hurdle the obstacles and give them counselling?" She asked herself many questions oh God! They were grieving for their father in jail. What a cruel human being was I?

She began to curse herself.

She was left feeling exposed and vulnerable for a few minutes.

She sat sobbed for sometime when she heard a loud call from Visakha.

"Shama, come here for a minute. I want to talk to you." She said aloud. Shama got down from the tree branch and rushed towards Visakha.

"Shama, we're leaving next week. You're going to leave the country next month. We're all going to separate. Only a few days left for our being together. We must make use of these days for enjoyment and merry making. It's not good to sit alone and brood over unnecessary things. We have to face our unavoidable life situations very boldly and with cheer and happiness. What's the matter that makes you so sad and moody? Your father came home after two years. Don't you have any love for him? Why do you always stay away from him? He's asking Kamini "Where's my daughter? And you're sitting here and swinging.

Come in Shama, and taste this pudding. Grandpa's calling you. He wants to feed you pudding with his hands.

Poor grandpa after a month he'll be left alone in this big house.

We requested him to come with us to Bombay. But he is too stubborn to change his views and ways of life.

Shama got excited and said with her eyes popped out of her head.

"Auntie, if you all agree I'll stay here with grandpa. Let the governess teach me as I don't want to continue my study in the Sacred Heart. Grandpa will be very happy to have me with him. Otherwise I'll be down in the dumps." She pleaded Visakha.

Visakha turned red with anger.

"Don't be so childish, Shama. Have you lost your senses? What are you talking about? Your father came here to take you there. Your parents have got high expectations of you. They want you to be get educated in a highly reputed school in America. Your father had already booked a seat in a famous secondary school near his hospital. Even grandpa won't allow you to spoil your life. Shed your foolish wish and try to accept the reality and please don't take the wind out of our sails."

While Visakha was turning to go in she heard the mellifluous voice of Miley near. "Good afternoon, doctor auntie."

Visakha welcomed her.

"Good afternoon, Miley. Come in my child." Said Visakha very affectionately.

"To the main building, auntie? Is it allowable for us to enter there? If Kamini aunt see me, she'll go into hysterics and beat me to death. I want Shama. I want to tell her something very important." Miley requested Visakha.

Shama took Miley to the outhouse and shut themselves away in a room while they were talking.

"Come on Miley what's the matter?" Shama asked anxiously.

"I'm going to stay with my grand parents in Ooty after the new year celebrations. I'll continue my education in the same school where my brother is studying. I'm very happy to leave the good for nothing Sacred Heart' with their rubbish job oriented studies and the teachers' Indian English. The teaching is as dull as ditch water and the education system is going down the tubes. I got the T.C yesterday. When are you travelling to the USA, Shama?

I thought of going to Ooty because your absence here will make my life miserable. I've to go a few days early to acclimatize myself to the cold there. Nothing you talked about your journey, your father, and about your future plan. "Miley breathed.

Shama was about to say that she did not want to leave grandpa and her bosom friends there when she heard a knock on the door. Shama jumped up and ran towards the door.

She opened it and saw to her surprise her mother holding a silver glass of sweet rice gruel mixed with raisins and cashew nuts and waiting.

Her lit up face with smiling eyes sweeten the minds of the children and Miley came running towards her like a beautiful butterfly to accept her offer.

"Miley, my child, forgive me for calling you 'nasrani' whenever I saw you with Shama, I have a fetish about cleanliness. You're welcome to the main building. I'm going to live in a cosmopolitan country where there is no caste or creed variability. Visakha conveyed your comments to me. That's why I myself came to invite you. I have a request for you Miley. Please advise your friend to be happy over the decision of her father to take us with him to America. She doesn't like leaving her friends and grandpa. It was her grandpa who forced his son to take his family with him and live together." Kamini patted Miley's hands with great expectations and chucked her under her chin. Miley saw a different kettle of fish. She said politely. "I too am going away from here to Ooty for my further studies. Cornelia may be an emigrant in the near future. Lady Mary is a woman of her word. So Shama too must get ready for her departure with an emollient decision. Please don't worry about her auntie. I'll take her to her father very soon. Please be riding high, Auntie, as far as Shama's consent is concerned."

Miley took Shama to her father. She ran to her father's stretched out arms and he cuddled his daughter as if she were an infant to him.

Miley's eyes were filled with tears of joy and contentment.

She felt sad over their separation. She thought that their blissful days are ended.

Shama and Miley looked at each other as if they were searching for something unknown in the depth of their minds.

With the permission of their parents they crossed the Anjengo backwater in Miley's small punt to meet Cornelia.

They decided to go to grandfather to get some solace. So Shama, Miley and Cornelia visited him. He was very glad to meet the trident.

"Hello, my little cherubs. How're you?"

"We're, fine uncle. Thank you very much." Said Miley. The children looked dejected since they came to know of their leaving home and study in different schools. They had pre departure jitters.

There were no way to escape from the reality. "We're going to go to different directions, grandpa. Is there a chance to get rid of this situation? You're a wise man. We came here to get good advise from you." Cornelia enquired of Grandpa.

Shama said in an undertone.

"I'm worrying about your loneliness in our absence here, grandpa. Why don't you go with Visakha auntie or with us to America. How can you get along without anybody here to help you grandpa? I wish I were with you! We'll be the happiest persons in the whole world then. Please tell my father to leave me with you in this ancestral home."

Grandpa's face was flushed with anger.

"What nonsense are you talking Shama?"

What about your future?

Where do you get a good education in this locality? Your friends are leaving you within a short time.

Where has your rationalistic approach of life gone? Now you talk like a silly girl. I haven't ever expected such an outlook on life from a girl like you."

Shama felt as if she were so idiotic in her way of talking.

"Sorry, grandpa. I said it because I love you more than I love my own father. Now I understood my mistake. No more in the doldrums. I'll not take the wind out of anybody's sails."

"We came here to get your blessing uncle. Miley and Shama are leaving shortly. My case is something that I cannot be sure about. If I am here I will look after you as my own grandfather unless there's caste barrier." Cornelia expressed herself delighted.

Oh, come on my girl. Have courage to face all sorts of difficult situations in our lives. Your parting is a must and you should study well and try to pave the way to a well settled life in future. May God bless you three to become the real gems!

Corne, you're savant and savoir faire of the trident. You may set sail for England by March. Lady Mary wrote to me that she was making all arrangements there for your emigration. I hope you can reach a high position in life.

I promise you, corne, that I'll surely help your father and your siblings in your absence and I've invited Lazar and children to occupy the dispensary building and give me company when I am left alone here.

Your brothers and sisters are very good company to me at this age."

Hearing this Shama felt a little jealous of Alex, Joseph, Mary and Lily.

On January 8th a long black chauffeur driven limousine was seen parked in the front yard of the main building to fetch the family of Shiva.

Grandpa was grieving in his heart for his second son who had not come to see him after a long period of his jail term.

He wished a lot to get a glimpse of him but he suppressed his feelings and very happily got ready to see off his daughter-in-law and his grandchildren. The chauffeur then handed over Shiva's letter to him.

Shiva could not come to see his father as he was very busy in Bombay with his official as well as family dealings. He wanted to furnish his new house allotted to him by the government.

He wrote a long letter to his father describing his painful experiences in prison and about his expounding on the new government's new policies.

"Father, I want to see you soon. After settling everything here I'll come to you. I'll stay with you for two weeks. We can enjoy a lot then.

I even wish that you would be with me in Bombay and give company to my two girls, Gaya and Gauri. You must give your love to them too like that you showers lavishly on Shama. They desperately want you to be with them. But that is beyond my wildest dreams.

Anyway I'll be there in February."

The letter took a load off his mind and grandpa became cheerful and wrote a reply to his son and handed it over to Visakha to deliver it to him.

"Tell him I'm craving to see him and to hold him tight to my breast. I expect his arrival and I am filled with a lot of longing to see him and hear his voice. Vishnu and family will leave for the U.S.A. on March 2nd. Can you and children come along with him once again to see them off? I'll be in great happiness if I can see you all together under this roof again, the first time after the demise of my Lakshmi, your loving mother-in-law. Lakshmi's spirit could be solaced by that sight.

Visakha showed her respect by touching his feet and promised him that they would accompany her husband.

"Father, your wish is perfectly plausible and we'll surely come with your son again to meet you and also to see off Vishnu brother and family. There's no change in that. I assure you."

People on either bank of the backwater arrived there to see their loving doctor off. Miley and Cornelia were there to say goodbye to Gaya and Gauri.

Cornelia presented Visakha with a new hand sewn sweater.

The doctor gave her a warm kiss in return.

They shook hands with Gaya and Gauri and wished them a very happy journey. Grandpa stood there with his eyes full of tears until the limousine disappeared from view.

On January tenth Miley was getting ready to leave for Ooty.

Shama and Cornelia bid Miley adieu.

It was a heart-rending scene. Even the guests were seen wiping their tears from their eyes when they witnessed the pathetic sight of the children hugging together and whimpering wildly. They had a tearful parting there.

No one could make them stay cool, calm and collected.

At last Miley's father put a consoling arm around their shoulders and appealed to them to take life as it came. "I'm sorry you're not happy about your parting but you'll just have to lump it."

Shama and Cornelia took Miley off to her car and the driver opened the door for her parents to enter. Miley was crying as Shama and Cornelia waved goodbye to her.

Shama's parents were busy packing bags and suitcases. Some of the household goods were packed in boxes and shipped to the US. The servants packed some food for them.

It was bedlam at the house in the morning of their departure.

Shiva arrived home with his family a week before.

Grandfather's enthusiasm knew no bounds. The members of the family as well as the servants and other workers in the house were in a mood of merrymaking. They were exuberant to see the family reunion.

Shama sat in a comer and thought about her future school, her companions, new friends and the strange circumstances that she had to face.

Cornelia sat home feeling an ugly and terrible loneliness. Her friends left her.

She felt groggy and lay down. She was not able to see her intimate friend off. Sometimes she might burst into tears and did not want to make a scene there.

Shama asked Miley's punt man to take her to Cornelia. While the puntman was getting ready to start the punt, Shama saw Alex running towards her.

"Sister conveys you her prayers and leave taking because she cannot face the painful departure. She is lying down on the hard floor of the room and crying her eyes out."

Somebody from the house called Shama aloud to come and get into the Limousine. It was Uncle Shiva who was going to take them to the Madras airport.

Seeing the hurly-burly in Shama's compound Alex said in a hurry.

"Sister I wish you good luck and a very happy foreign life on my behalf and on behalf of my sister, your Corne."

Shama burst into tears and ran towards her house where everyone was bidding one's adieu to the departing family.

Final examination in seventh form started in March Sixteen in the Sacred Heart English Middle School in Anjengo.

Cornelia went alone to write the exam.

The question papers were so easy that even a fourth form student in the British curriculum could get a score of hundred out of hundred.

Almost all English students left the school except a few who would also get their T.C after the annual exam.

After the annual examination Cornelia, under the aegis of Shama's grandpa, started to learn Hindi under a qualified teacher hailed from Delhi. His Hindi Institute was in a place called Kayikara. She went on foot to study there- She learned Hindi from scratch in six weeks.

The result of the annual examination was published in April.

Cornelia was awarded with the best pupil award and a gold medal for her extra curricular talents.

The Vicar of St. Peter's church along with the teachers and students of St. Joseph's School arranged a glamorous function to pay Cornelia a compliment for being selected by the Cultural Society of St. Joseph's Teens as the Teens Little Beauty Princess of Anjengo and to award her a crown and a gold medallion.

Lazar and his sons and daughters attended the function and he was praised by the chief guest for having a daughter like Cornelia.

Cornelia prayed silently to Jesus for giving her such a great blessings and boons. Cornelia approached grandpa first with the medallion and the crown of flowers.' He put his hands on her forehead and blessed her.

Cornelia had not yet received any message from Lady Mary till May last.

So grandfather advised Lazar to arrange for her eighth form admission in an English Medium High School in Trivandrum.

By the time grandpa wrote a long letter to Lady Mary enquiring about Cornelia's sponsorship and emigration details.

"Here, schools are functioning from June Second onwards. If there is any delay or difficulty in her emigration process let me know as early as possible. We don't want to miss her academic year. Anyway we are going to put her in a boarding school in Trivandrum run by a Scottish Academy." Grandpa ended his letter with a very nice leave taking.

On May fifteenth grandpa received a letter from Lady Mary. She replied that she was not in a position to take Cornelia to England because she got spliced with a naval officer in Ireland.

She apologized for her inability to help Cornelia. She sent a letter of apology to Lazar and Cornelia.

So grandpa took it as his responsibility to arrange for her high school admission in an eminent English School in Trivandrum as there was none in the immediate vicinity.

Thus Cornelia had to separate from her father and her siblings for the first time to mould and colour her life.

The little children of Anjengo's separation was inevitable.

They may have been leading their successful lives elsewhere.

Their reunion is eagerly awaited by the people of Anjengo, the blabbering backwater and the rootin-tootin Arabian Sea.